All Roads Lead to Terror

This Lawless Land
Book I

Richard Schiver

Abiss Books
Copyright ©2015 Richard Schiver
All rights reserved.
ISBN - 978-1-951552-06-0

Dedication

For my grandchildren.

Corey, Tyler, Destiny, Kamryn,
Anthony, Aidyn Amyah,
Madisyn, Liam, and Grayson

They offer hope for the future.

1

It's been said every journey begins with a single step. Their journey began, as many do, with a desire to do the right thing coupled with a heathy dose of adolescent bravado. At the Bluffs, the idea seemed pretty straight forward. Follow the group that kidnapped the kids and take them back. But now, with the security of the fence miles behind them, Meat struggled as the first of many doubts surfaced.

What if they knew they were being followed?

What if they were waiting for them around the next bend?

What if the kids weren't alive?

What would they do then?

Not wanting to fall into the trap of chasing his tail with his worries, he turned his attention to the sign scattered all around him. An overturned rock here, the shaft of a weed bent at an unnatural angle there, a pile of decaying leaves disturbed by hasty steps. Small signs that alone meant nothing, yet when taken as a whole wrote a tale of hurried desperation. The group passed this way less than two days before.

He was relieved when he picked out several partial prints of booted feet. The kids were still alive. How much longer was anybody's guess so they better hurry if they hoped to rescue them.

With the evening sun to his back his shadow stretched out before him, pointing east, into an unknown land. They had a few hours left before night forced them to stop. Time better spent gaining on their quarry.

All Roads Lead to Terror

From the forest on both sides of the railroad tracks came the incessant chatter of life. New growth offset the chill of winters recent passing with spring's promise of rebirth. Confirmation that life would go on no matter what, following the cycles of the seasons that replaced the calendars of old. Time was no longer measured in weeks, or months. The coming and going of the sun and moon, and the passing of the seasons was all they needed to know.

Meat brushed off his knees as he stood and looked back at the other three with him. Window had settled into a kneeling position, fading as best he could into the trees along his side of the tracks. His features hidden beneath a wide-brimmed hat. Ten yards behind Window, on the opposite side of the tracks, Einstein let his pack fall to the ground before following himself with a tired groan.

It was Einstein's first trip beyond the fence, and it showed. Not only in the size of the pack he carried, which had been lightened the morning of their second day when he abandoned his tent, but by his appearance. In contrast to the others Einstein still carried the baby fat of his youth, lending him a pudginess they lacked.

Meat and the other two had more experience outside the fence. They traveled light, carrying only the bare necessities. A sleeping blanket or two, a change of clothes, ammunition, and of course food. Rabbit and deer jerky along with a few potatoes. Anything else they needed they took from the land around them. Supplementing their diet with what nature provided.

Meat shook his head as he signed. Twenty yards behind Einstein, Billie-Bob, the youngest member of their group, walked the rail with a predatory grace. The edges of his long canvas jacket danced around his legs. His head bouncing to a beat only he could hear. He carried himself with an ease the others lacked. In sharp contrast to this economy of motion, his mouth was running a mile a minute as he recited a monologue only he was privy to, unaware the others had stopped.

"Billie-Bob," Meat shouted as he approached.

Billie-Bob jumped, startled, his young face breaking into a wide smile when he spotted Meat's approach. At eleven he possessed an ability that by its nature made him a loner. A natural born sniper with a target sense that made hitting any target second nature. No matter the distance, whether moving or stationary, he knew right where to place the crosshairs for a kill shot.

It was a talent useful for keeping the meat lockers full of wild game. But the quarry they sought now was far more dangerous than any of the wildlife they encountered, and Meat worried if the boy was up to the task. It was one thing to drop a fleeing deer, quite another to pull the trigger on a human being, and the walking dead didn't count. They were already dead, and everybody shot at them.

"Kapitan." Billie-Bob snapped to attention and whipped his hand around in a quick salute. The smile, though open and friendly, failed to reach eyes that carried a preternatural stillness. Eyes that had seen more than a child his age should. They all carried that same look, a careworn expression, a thousand-yard stare so out of place on faces so young.

"What did I ask you to do?" Meat said as he neared.

Billie-Bob's eyes widened as he looked around. "Watch our rear?"

"And what are you doing?"

Billie-Bob rolled his eyes as he looked over Meat's shoulder at Einstein, who watched from his reclining position. "I thought I was watching our rear?"

"You have to look behind us every once in a while, make sure no one's sneaking up on us."

"Right, got it, I'll take care of that. Hey, did I ever tell you about the zombie that went to the whorehouse?" Billie-Bob said with a snicker.

"Only about a hundred times." Meat shook his head.

"He wanted his money back because he couldn't get it up. He had DD, a dead dick." Billie-Bob finished with a guffaw. "Get it? DD? Dead dick?" He slapped Meat on the shoulder with a hearty laugh.

Meat shrugged and walked away as Billie-Bob chuckled in merriment. It was the only thing he could do. He'd known the boy for several years and if anything could be said about him, he was scripting his own life.

Like the rest of them, with the exception of Einstein, Billie-Bob and his twin brother showed up outside the fence one morning. No one knew where they came from, or what circumstances brought them to this isolated place. Some things were too painful to talk about. Meat knew this all too well. He had his own secrets to keep him up at night.

Meat's journey to Bremo Bluff, or The Bluffs, as they liked to call it, had been fraught with danger. He'd grown up with a group of adults always on the move. Never staying in one spot for longer than a few days. Keeping one step ahead of the walking dead, and other groups of survivors searching for a safe place that no longer existed.

Meat reached Einstein and gave him a hand getting to his feet. "Everything all right?"

Einstein nodded. Sweat stained the collar of his shirt and darkened the fabric beneath his armpits. He mopped his forehead with a handkerchief. "How much longer?"

"Another two, three hours before we call it a night." The look of dismay on Einstein's face told Meat everything he needed to know. While he had a tremendous amount of respect for what the boy knew, he'd spent too much time with the books and not enough time playing. He was soft. But this trip might toughen him up.

"Are you getting enough water?"

Einstein nodded as he put his hand on Meat's shoulder. "I want to thank you for letting me come along, but man, this trip is killing me."

"You'll be all right." Meat turned to resume his place at point, stopping next to Window, who watched the trail ahead.

Billie-Bob returned to his monologue and Window shook his head as the ghost of a smile tugged at the corner of lips not accustomed to any measure of gaiety. "Does he ever shut up?" Window's hand rested on the butt of the revolver protruding from the leather holster slung low on his hip. He was the quiet one, always watching, ever aware of his surroundings. The .44 in his holster a necessarily constant companion.

"Only when he's sleeping."

"Well he better, or I'll make him set up camp a mile away from the rest of us."

"We're gonna have to pick up the pace. The sign's still strong, I don't want to give it a chance to get washed away." Meat nodded at the darkening clouds to the east. A storm was brewing, with dense black clouds piling up in the distance. As if that part of the world were angry at their intrusion.

They set out, Einstein groaning as he shouldered his burden once again, and Meat picked up the pace as he raced the storm ahead of them.

All Roads Lead to Terror

Fourteen years earlier, the world changed when a virus reanimated the recently deceased. Their numbers multiplied, catching the living population off guard, especially in the cities where the walking dead ruled and the options for those still alive dwindled.

When it seemed all hope was lost, decomposition began thinning the ranks of the zombies as muscle and flesh fell prey to the natural process of decay. Even as their ranks thinned, death strode among the living, creating reinforcements for the dwindling masses of the undead that severely cut the world's population.

In this new reality, standard medical care was a thing of the past as hospitals and clinics had been overwhelmed in the initial outbreak. Even the simplest of cuts could become a death sentence if not cared for in a timely manner.

The virus was still present. Where it came from and how it spread remained mysteries as the greatest minds were wiped out in the initial outbreak. Pushed to the brink of extinction, mankind continued his struggle to survive in this new world.

Before the outbreak, the co-generation plant at the Bluffs was connected to the national electrical grid. In the early days, those with foresight took charge, cutting the connection with the grid and saving the plant as they established a fenced compound around the Bluff. Two of its four turbines still used coal, so when the flow of natural gas stopped, they switched to them.

Knowing the odds of survival over the long haul was tied to their population, they welcomed survivors with open arms. As the population grew, the number of skilled workers increased, adding to the availability of safe housing and products that helped make daily life a little easier.

The growing population put a strain on local resources but provided ample manpower to staff scavenging crews who would scour the world beyond the fence, contacting other camps and establishing trade for what they lacked. Every direction they explored had proven fruitful with the exception of anything to the east. Over the past four years, three crews vanished into the unknown country that lay between their compound and the Atlantic Ocean. An area modern man had inhabited the longest.

Based on the map he carried, the city of Richmond, which had once been the capital of Virginia, lay to the east. It was the direction the trail they followed ran. Vanishing into the growing night as towering storm clouds piled atop one another in the distance. Brief flashes of lightning illuminated their depths as the scent of freshly fallen rain came to them, carried on a steady breeze. Another smell intruded, teasing him with its familiarity only to fade away before returning stronger than before.

Meat lifted his hand, calling a halt as he knelt. The others stopped in their tracks with Window mimicking his actions, to offer as little a target as possible to any potential marksmen ahead of them. Einstein and Billie-Bob stood where they stopped, their heads on a swivel as they looked around.

Meat motioned for them to move up to his position.

Einstein and Window knelt on either side as Billie-Bob watched over Meat's shoulder.

"Can you smell that?" Meat said.

The others sniffed at the air.

"Wood smoke," Window said, and Meat nodded.

"I've been catching whiffs of it for the past half hour. It comes and goes on the breeze, its growing stronger, so we're getting close to whoever it is."

"Are we catching up with them?" Einstein asked.

"Where's it coming from?" Billie Bob said.

Meat held up his hand and sniffed the air, his actions reminiscent of a predator searching for its prey. He stood and turned in a slow circle, his eyes closed, as he sampled the air. Fresh and sweet, with a hint of decay from the nearby river, an ever-present mustiness that accompanied the slow-moving waters. Mother Nature had washed away the old smells, the ones he'd grown up with.

Their memory lingered, the ever-present stench of rotting flesh, of decay and destruction that became an integral part of his childhood memories. It was an odor he would not soon forget. He caught another whiff of the wood smoke filtered through the trees, carried on a gentle breeze that stirred the leaves around them.

"To the north." He opened his eyes and moved to the dense forest crowded close to the railroad tracks. It had been fourteen years since they had been last maintained. It had been that long since anything had been looked after, and Mother Nature was reclaiming what was once hers. Even though it was overgrown, the path the old railroad tracks followed was still visible, a healing scar on a wild world.

"Cover our rear." Einstein turned and followed Meat into the forest. Billie-Bob glanced left and then right, his mouth working silently as he mimicked Einstein's words.

"Always telling me what to do." Billie-Bob gazed at the forest and whispered to himself, "They roared their terrible roars, and gnashed their terrible teeth, and rolled their terrible eyes, and showed their terrible claws." With a final look around, he too vanished into the forest.

2

Meat moved through the forest with an ease earned over years of exploring the wilds around Bremo Bluffs. He followed a straight line with Einstein and Window fanning out to both flanks. He didn't know what to expect. It could be a few of the raiding party hanging back, waiting for them to pass before following with the hope of catching them in a crossfire. Or it could be another survivor traveling the empty roads in search of a safe haven.

Near a clearing, he stopped and knelt. Ahead of him a solitary house stood surrounded by empty fields. It was a ramshackle old structure, the paint peeling from its outer walls to expose the weathered wood beneath. Several of the windows were covered with boards, and the roof of the porch sagged in the middle.

A small trickle of smoke rose from the only chimney.

He motioned for the others to stay back and signaled Billie-Bob to get ready. He stopped when he spotted a barn with a corral along one side. Two people stood in the corral, side by side at the fence, the top part of their bodies rocking back and forth in time with one another.

Each wore a dress, the hem covered in mud that had dried in spots. They were barefoot, their hands resting on the top rail of the fence as they watched the house with unwavering gazes.

Cautiously, Meat moved along the side of the corral. The women remained unaware as he approached, his eyes never leaving their backs, and the house beyond, watching for signs of movement at the windows.

He noticed that they both had stopped rocking, their backs becoming ramrod straight, yet their hands remained in place on the top rail. As he got closer, one of the women turned with a growl. The flesh of her face was gray, her eyes white with cataracts, filthy teeth hidden behind snarling lips.

They'd been turned, Meat faded back from the corral, the other woman followed the first, staggering to where Meat stood, their hands outstretched as they sought the comfort his body could provide.

"Stop it, both of you." A shout came from the porch of the worn structure and a large man stood in the open doorway. A rifle rested in the crook of his elbow. The women turned at the sound of the man's voice, staggering to the fence of the corral where they watched him. He stepped out of the shadows, a long salt and pepper beard resting against his chest.

"I see you out there," the man said, "hiding in the bushes. Come out with your hands up." He settled the butt of the rifle against his shoulder and took aim through the telescopic sight.

Meat stood up, his hands held at shoulder height, his fingers spread wide. It would serve as a signal for Billie-Bob to hold fire. Meat was confident he was even now sighting through the scope of his M24, a present from his surrogate parents, the man on the porch in his sights. As long as Meat's hands remained open, the man on the porch would live. The moment he closed either hand into a fist, Billie-Bob would take his shot.

It was a signal they worked out before venturing beyond the fence. In this old new world, it was not only the zombies you needed to worry about. Other survivors, struggling to live themselves, presented a greater risk, as the only law you had to fall back upon was whatever weapons you carried.

"Drop your gun," the man on the porch said, the muzzle of his rifle unwavering as Meat gazed down its length.

"I can't do that," Meat said.

"What do you want?"

"I'm looking for someone, a group of kids."

"A group of kids?" The muzzle wavered. He'd hit a nerve.

"They kidnapped several children from the compound where I live, we want them back."

"What place are you talking about? Where do you live?"

"I can't tell you that." Meat was about to close his hand into a fist, worried the man on the porch was getting tired and might accidentally squeeze off a shot. The man lowered his rifle and sat down on the top step. "I tried to stop them."

"Who?" Meat approached the house.

"Those kids you're looking for, they're not children. Oh, they're small all right, and they look like kids, but they're not. They're savages. That's what threw Maggie off. One of them came out of the forest several days ago, pretending like he was hurt. Maggie went to help him, and the others, they came out of the forest. She tried to run." A solitary tear traced a wet path down his cheek as he relived the moment. "She ran, and Shelly tried to help, but there was too many of them."

"Who are Maggie and Shelly?"

The man looked at him, the sorrow of the world resting upon his slumped shoulders. "My wife and daughter." His gaze drifted to the two women in the corral. "I know I need to take care of them, to do the right thing. I can't bring myself to do it, not to the woman I've spent my life with, or the child I've sworn to protect."

It all made sense and Meat signaled for the others to come up. As they emerged from the forest, the old man spotted them and became alarmed. "What do you want?"

"We're not here to hurt you, I promise. We smelled the wood smoke and came to see what was going on."

The man reached for his rifle and Meat put his hand on the barrel.

"I don't have anything you want."

"We're not after anything, old man, we want to find those kids, get our own kids back. Which way did they go?" he asked, trying to get the man's mind off of his current line of thought.

"East," the old man said as he watched the other three approach.

"We can help you," Meat said, "if you need us to."

"How? You're nothing more than a child yourself."

Meat shrugged. Some people still held onto their old beliefs, unwilling to accept the reality in which they lived. Judging by the man's age, he had lived before the awakening, so he still clung to the viewpoint that children should not concern themselves with adult matters. "Your wife and daughter, they should have peace."

The man's eyes widened as he leaned back to escape Meat's observation. "What do you know about anything? You're only a kid."

"I know they need to be put to rest. Every one of us learned that at a very young age. The only cure for what they have is a bullet to the brain."

"That's my wife and daughter you're talking about, boy." The man's hand moved to the rifle and Meat rested his foot on the barrel, keeping it in place as the old man looked at him with water-rimmed eyes.

"Window, you know what needs to be done." Meat never took his eyes off of the old man. "You should have done this sooner. It's not your wife and daughter anymore, you know that. Why else would you be keeping them locked up in the corral?"

"Shut up, dammit."

"Does she sleep with you at night? Do you tuck in your daughter with a kiss?"

"Shut the fuck up, you bastard. What do you know about anything?"

"I know I can't leave them as they are. I know somewhere deep down inside they're begging to be released."

The old man jumped when the first shot shattered the stillness of the day. Several birds took flight, startled from their roost, flapping away with angry cries as a second shot followed the first. They faded into the distance like thunder rolling away to silence. From the north came the faint sound of an engine growling, its tone rising and then falling before fading away.

What's that? Meat wondered before the man shoved him aside and raced down the steps, his boots throwing up clouds of dust as he crossed the bare ground.

"Maggie, Shelly." The old man's voice cracked with emotion. Einstein stood in his way, and Meat motioned for him to let the old man go. Sitting down on the top step, he waited as the old man's cries came from the direction of the corral. The others joined him.

"Are we gonna bury them?" Window said.

"When he's ready." Meat waited as late afternoon slipped into early evening. If need be, they'd spend the night here before continuing their journey. He knew Window was anxious to get going, he was not one who liked to wait on anyone or anything. Meat understood it would be best to help the old man once he realized what they'd done was best for his wife and daughter.

After an hour, the unmistakable sound of a shovel biting into the earth came from the corral. Together they crossed the yard to help the old man lay his family to rest.

3

In a world without electricity, night came fast. After burying the old man's family, they returned to the front porch and prepared to move on before setting up camp. The old man, who had exhausted most of his sorrow before they arrived, would not hear of it. After introducing himself he insisted they stay for the night.

His name was Gregory, and before the awakening he'd been the manager of a home improvement store outside Richmond. When the shit hit the fan, he took his wife and daughter to his cabin in the mountains west of Richmond to ride everything out. Unfortunately, the zombies turned out to be the least of his troubles. They'd been found and driven from their home by a group of men and women better armed, and far more savage than he could bring himself to be

Sitting around the kitchen table, with several candles providing their only light, Gregory finished his story and looked at each of them expectantly, his hands folded on the table before him.

"You lived in the world before all this happened?" Einstein said.

"We were in our thirties when it happened, our daughter was five."

"You know about fast food and grocery stores, what were they like? Could you really get a whole meal in less than a minute?" Billie-Bob asked.

Gregory shrugged. "Absolutely. In the city, a fast food joint was on practically every corner."

"That's amazing. Man, I wish I could have seen that," Billie-Bob said.

"Where are you from?"

Window and Meat exchanged glances. Window tilted his head and Meat agreed. "We're from a place upriver called Bremo Bluff."

"I've heard of it," Gregory said. "Isn't there a co-generation plant there?"

"Yeah, we have electricity. We use it to make fresh water too," Billie-Bob said. Window scowled as Meat shrugged. They'd learned long ago to be cautious about what information they shared with strangers.

"What about libraries?" Meat said.

"What about them?"

"Do you know where one might be, one that hasn't been torched or destroyed?"

Gregory shook his head. "I'm sorry, libraries weren't at the top of my list of priorities when I was trying to protect my family. How do you know about libraries?"

"An old lady where I live, she has a room filled with books, they're story books, not real books you can learn anything from. She does have a set of encyclopedias from the fifties. She told me about libraries."

"You can read?"

"Of course. To live where we live, it's required. Everyone has a job to do to ensure the survival of the group, and you have to be able to read to follow instructions."

"Don't they have any other books?"

"Technical manuals for running the plant, how-to books about making things, those sorts of books. I'd like to read about our history, what the world was like before all this happened." Meat finished with a shrug.

"Do the children work?"

"Everyone has to work."

"Then why are you outside?"

"The parents of the children who had been kidnapped hired us to find them. They agreed to take on our jobs until our return."

"And if you don't?"

Meat smiled. "We've been going outside the fence for two years now, staying close, scavenging what we can find. We know the risks and I know the other three with me, I know what we're capable of. We'll return to The Bluffs with the children."

"What about the kids who took them? What do you plan to do to them?"

"Nothing if they stay out of our way."

"Why are you doing this? Are they paying you?"

Meat shook his head. "We're doing it because we want to help, and if we're successful, we may be able to convince the council to award us a scavenging slot."

"A scavenging slot?"

"There are scavenging teams that search for necessities beyond the fence. Each one is assigned a particular item to look for and bring back."

"You're doing this more for yourself then?"

"Not really. I mean, getting a slot would be nice, even if it wasn't available, we'd still do it.

"That's pretty altruistic of you."

"What does that mean?" Window said.

"It means we're generous," Meat said.

Window shrugged. "Speak for yourself. I'm in it to find more bullets and guns. You can never have too many guns."

"Don't mind Window, he hates zombies and practically everybody else.

"Why do they call him Window?"

"It's a nickname we came up with for him. His real name is Chris, but since he's so open about his past, he's as clear as a window."

"I take it you're being sarcastic."

"Absolutely." Meat smiled. "By the way, my name's Meat, that's Einstein on Window's left, and at the end of the table is Billie-Bob." Each of them in turn nodded.

"Whatever happened to regular names, you know like Don and Mark, Fred and Pete?" Gregory said with a bewildered expression.

"Einstein's real name is Arthur. Billie-Bob is one half of a set of twins. His name is Billie, and his brother's name is Bobbie. When they were younger, they would trade places with each other, so everyone started calling them Billie-Bob as they were never sure which of the twins they were really talking to."

"What's your real name?"

"I don't have one. According to the man who raised me I was born during the awakening. My mom didn't want me. Said I was nothing more than meat so that's what they started calling me, that or boy. I was never given a real name." Meat stopped as his emotions surged to the surface. Struggling to contain his tears he looked around the table and what he saw awakened his jealousy. Everyone at the table, aside from himself, had been raised by parents that loved them enough to give them a name. A name that would serve as a connection to their past. He had no past, most likely no future either.

"Are you all right?" Gregory placed his hand on Meat's arm.

"I'm okay." Meat got his emotions under control. "Besides, it fits. Aren't we all nothing more than walking bags of meat?"

"That's a pretty dismal view of the world."

"It's a pretty dismal world we live in."

"You'll get no argument from me," Gregory said.

"How did it happen?" Billie-Bob asked.

"How did what happen?"

"The awakening? They told us in class it was because of a virus. A company was trying to make a biological weapon that mutated into the virus. They never gave us any other details."

"I don't think anyone is sure what happened. I know it started in a small town outside Pittsburgh. Some said a train derailed and one of the tankers carrying government cargo ruptured. Others claimed a military transport plane crashed into the woods outside the city. Some believe it was tied to the Ebola virus that was out of control in South Africa. A few of the experts even claimed it was the result of radiation from a NASA probe falling back to earth.

"Whatever the reason most of the people fled from the area, carrying the virus that spread around the world. The next thing we knew, anyone who recently died woke up. Hospital morgues, funeral homes, places where the dead are stored, saw the dead attacking the living.

"Panic set in as people fled the cities. The government collapsed under the strain as the normal restraints of civilization crumbled, and it became a dog eat dog world. The undead were only half the problem. Survivalists and militia groups who'd been waiting for something like this to happen went on killing sprees. It was crazy. If you weren't dead or didn't belong to one of the groups that sprung up in the aftermath, you were a target."

"Like now," Meat said, "most of our problems come from survivors instead of the walking dead."

"Man's inhumanity to man. Throughout history man has been his own worst enemy."

"It's getting late. If we want to get started by first light, we need to get some sleep."

"There's plenty of floor space," Gregory said, "grab a spot."

"Do you have any objections to us sleeping in your barn?"

"No, I don't understand why."

"Call it a precaution. I'll take the first watch, Einstein you'll be second, Billie-Bob third, and Window, you can wake me for the last two hours."

"I can handle it."

"I know you can. I'll sit with you, keep you company."

"If that's what you want."

Meat nodded as he pushed himself away from the table. He stuck his hand out for Gregory. "It's been a pleasure and thank you for your hospitality."

"The pleasure was all mine. When do you plan on setting out in the morning?"

"Early, I'd like to be gone before the sun comes up."

The others pushed away from the table and crossed to the front door where they waited for Meat.

4

Three hundred and ninety miles north of the boys, near the border between New York and Pennsylvania, Jamie followed the blood trail of a deer. It was the deepest he'd ever gone into the forest that stretched for miles across rolling hills in every direction. Everything around him was fresh, new, unfamiliar in a way that disturbed him.

Untouched, was the thought that came to mind. Massive trunks marched away into the distance, supporting towering trees that had been mature when the nation was born. They made him feel small, insignificant, his life a brief moment when compared to theirs. He glanced back the way he'd come. At the cuts he left in his wake as he marked his path with a hatchet. The sight was satisfying. Long after he was gone, they would remember his passage in the wounds he left behind.

The blood trail of the deer he'd wounded was becoming spotty at best, yet he pushed on, driven by a combination of irritation and fear. His anger at missing such a good shot coupled with a fear of his father, and what he might think of him.

Don't let em suffer, his father's words came, accompanied by the memory of a slap across the face for being too stupid to shoot a deer properly. Followed by an endless trek through the forest, his father cursing every step of the way. A couple of times, Jamie was overwhelmed by a desire to blow the bastard's head off with his rifle.

He knew he wouldn't.

He was terrified his father would know what he was about to do and turn on him at the last moment. From experience he knew how brutal his father could be. Trying something stupid like that would result in his own death, if he was lucky. With the possibility his father would leave him, hurt and bleeding in the forest alone.

Even now he suspected he was watching from the other side, shaking his head as he questioned the intelligence of his offspring. The animal didn't deserve a lingering death and if he'd been more focused on the task at hand, he'd be at home right now with the meat cooling in the shed.

Thoughts of his dad reminded him of what they'd done to him when Jamie was a boy. He enjoyed the memory as he relived the moment they dragged him from the house like a rabid dog. His mother was no better, the only difference being he could withstand her beatings better than he could his old man's. She wasn't as strong as his dad and he fixed her too, in time. Thankfully they lived away from the others and the smell had not alerted anyone that something was wrong.

Movement between the trees drew his attention and he focused on that spot. It came again, accompanied by a thrashing in the blanket of leaves covering the forest floor. He spotted the deer on its side struggling to get to its feet. Dropping to one knee he sighted on the animal, timing the movement of its head as it struggled.

It's gonna be hell dragging him back. The forest behind the animal had grown much darker in the short period of time he'd settled into a firing position. *Might have to spend the night.* He shuddered at the thought, ill equipped as he was for a night in the forest. Spring may have recently sprung, but the night still carried the memory of winter's recent passing.

He'd have to be more careful in the future. Ammunition was growing scarcer by the day. Every gun shop and retailer within a thirty-mile radius of his hometown had been stripped bare after the awakening. The only place to get any would be Ted's hardware on main street, and his prices had tripled recently.

Thinking of Ted sparked another memory. He thought about Penny and what he'd like to do to her. They'd grown up together during the worst days of the awakening, or what Reverend Wood called the rapture.

God has called the dead home, and the rest of the sinners have been left behind to make amends for our wicked ways. The Reverend's words whispered through his mind and he smiled. Reverend Woods was a fool, as was anyone else who believed the drivel he spewed, his mother included. She'd taken his words hook, line, and sinker.

Ever since Ted's dad gave him the store on main street they'd grown apart. Penny playing them against one another, driving the wedge even deeper as she paraded around town in short skirts and halters teasing them both with carnal promises.

Not much remained of the world as it had once been. Corydon Township, where he lived, was only a few miles from the New York state line and changed little after the awakening. Surrounded by miles of uninhabited wilderness, insulated from the worst effects of the awakening, the survivors came together to form a small community that viewed all travelers with suspicion. Their remote location ensured their survival while forcing them to become even more self-reliant than before.

He was taking up the slack on the trigger when from the forest behind the deer, four men on horseback emerged from the trees.

One moment the forest was empty, and in the next they appeared. Jamie lowered his rifle and eased to his right, rubbing his eyes as he dropped to a prone position to watch them.

They became aware of the deer thrashing on the ground nearby. The two on the right drew their revolvers and turned to face the sound as the other two slipped from their mounts and moved silently through the forest. One of the men on foot reached the dying deer. He said something to the others that put them at ease.

A shot rang out as the deer was put out of its misery. Jamie jumped at the sound, stirring the dead leaves around him, and one of the mounted riders swiveled his head to look in Jamie's direction. Their eyes locked and Jamie looked away from that cruel visage.

These men did not come in peace.

When he felt it was safe to do so he lifted his head to watch as one of the dismounted riders threw the carcass of the deer across their horse's back. They were taking his food, and had it been anyone else he would have confronted them. What he'd seen in that mounted man's gaze silenced him.

They spoke among themselves, their voices low, their words indistinct as they rode by. Each horse a different color. White, red, black, and gray. The one he'd locked gazes with glanced in his direction and Jamie looked away. They knew he was there, yet they continued south as night filled the forest with deepening shadows.

Where did they come from? Where are they going? The questions chased one another through his mind as he emerged from his hiding place and approached the stand of trees they'd emerged from. He became aware of a faint humming that seemed to be coming from the stand of ancient trees. Felt more than heard, the humming grew stronger with every step he got closer. He realized the sound was keeping time with his beating heart, rising and falling with a faint rhythm that marked the passing of the seconds.

He reached out, stepping back with a cry when his hand vanished. He heard the riders come to a stop and he glanced back to make sure they had not circled around behind him. The forest was empty, and he turned to the stand of trees. Curiosity forced him to stick his hand back into that void and a soothing warmth flowed over his fingers, in sharp contrast to the chill of the night around him.

Where does it go?

He reached deeper, his arm vanishing to the shoulder, wrapped in a luxurious warmth that lured him forward. As that calming sensation lulled him into a relaxed state, he panicked and tried to pull his arm back. Something grabbed his arm and pulled him toward the void. He tried to back away, digging in his heels, but it was no use, and he was dragged across to the other side.

A cacophony of noise surrounded him as the world was turned upon itself. The trees folded over, twisted and mutilated, as a dark red light bled through the spaces between them. For a moment he floated, detached from the world around him, afraid he might drift away into this strange nothingness. He landed with a jarring crash that sent him sprawling to the ground, his hands sliding across coarse stone.

The sun burned against his back, the ground beneath him unyielding. The air filled with an acrid scent that left a charred taste in the back of his throat.

Where am I?

He lifted his head and looked around. Several stunted trees grew nearby, pine by the look of them. Their trunks twisted into unnatural shapes, their branches nearly bare, a few small sprigs of green at the tip of each. He pushed himself to his feet to find he stood upon a mountaintop. Spinning around he came face to face with a blank stone wall, the striation of ancient upheavals marring its surface.

Behind him the mountaintop looked out upon a valley filled with a vast white castle that sparkled in the sunlight. Slender spires reached for the clouds burnished with the red hues of a setting sun. Birds flew around the tops where long flags waved, tiny black dots against the emptiness of the sky.

Am I in heaven?

Around him the ground was bare stone with a few twisted pine trees clinging to life in the narrow cracks criss crossing its surface. The only thing that stood out was the slab of stone behind him. Stepping closer he felt that familiar humming and when he reached out, he was rewarded with his hand vanishing from sight. It was the way home to the world he knew, and without hesitation he stepped into the stone.

His head spinning with vertigo he crashed to the floor of the forest and lay for a moment breathing deeply of the familiar scent of home. He recalled the four men on horseback as one of the passages the reverend used to read from the bible came to mind.

"So, I looked, and behold, a pale horse. And the name of him who sat on it was Death, and Hades followed with him."

Are they the four horsemen?

Was the awakening really the rapture like Reverend Wood said? Had God abandoned them? Were these the end times? Were the four men angels sent from heaven to bring an end to humanity?

All Roads Lead to Terror

There was only one way to find out, and Jamie followed their path as the forest drifted into darkness.

5

The smell of woodsmoke led Jamie to their camp and he eased into the hollow of a tree to watch them. Shivering he wrapped his arms about himself to conserve his warmth. He was not prepared for a night in the forest. When he left the house this morning, he believed he would be back no later than noon, so he packed light.

He should be at home now, in bed, but curiosity and the reverend's words compelled him to follow the strangers. He was afraid if he went home to gather supplies, he would lose them.

He doubted anyone would miss him when he failed to return. He and his parents rarely got along with their neighbors. After his father's demise he and his mother were tolerated by the community, but never included. Penny was probably with Ted right now, sharing his bed, fulfilling his fantasies while Jamie froze his ass off in the night.

Thoughts of Penny warmed him, and he smiled as he settled into his position. Lost in erotic thoughts featuring Penny he didn't hear the branch break behind him, nor the footstep stirring the leaves on the forest floor.

He did feel the muzzle of the pistol pressed behind his ear.

"Show me your hands," a gravelly voice came from the shadows behind him. He awakened to the realization he'd been a fool to follow these men. He should have left well enough alone.

The flesh of his face was stiff, his arms heavy with the cold as he struggled to pull them from around his chest to show they were empty.

"On your feet." The muzzle was pulled away from his head.

He struggled to stand, his thoughts once again straying to home and the safety it offered. It was too late now. The muscles of his legs contracted as he tried to stand, having been locked in one position for too long they refused to move freely. He knew if he didn't comply with the stranger's order, he'd be dead. As long as he was breathing there was a chance he'd survive.

Using the tree for support he pushed himself to his feet. His toes tingled with the renewed flow of blood as he stood unsteadily.

"Walk into the camp." The muzzle prodded his back, forcing him toward the fire and the warmth it provided.

"Are you one of the horsemen? Did you come from heaven?" Jamie said as he stumbled through the forest.

"Keep your hands where I can see them."

"Our reverend said it was the end times and the four horsemen would soon come to destroy mankind."

A hand dropped onto his shoulder to stop him.

"We're coming in." The voice shouted next to his ear and Jamie cringed.

He became aware of three shadows emerging from the darkness into the soft light of the fire. They were dressed alike, in homemade denim pants stuffed into high boots. Beneath their coats they wore leather vests adorned with assorted symbols and sigils that made no sense. From each of their hips hung a holster that contained a revolver with large wooden grips.

"Sit," the man on the other side of the fire said, pointing at a log next to the blaze. As he settled into his seat Jamie watched them gather at the edge of the forest to speak among themselves. Several times one would glance in his direction as they spoke. The warmth of the fire made it difficult for him to keep his eyes open and he struggled to stay awake as his fate was decided.

To his left the deer they'd taken hung upside down, strung up by its hind legs from between two trees. The glow of the fire reflected from dead eyes that watched his every move. Blood dripped from its snout, into a metal pot beneath its head. The pot appeared to be half full. His stomach rolled over as he gazed into the deer's dead eyes. A small part of him expected the deer to wink at him, knowing if it did, he'd run screaming into the forest.

"You know this world?"

The voice drove him awake and he opened his eyes to find the four men watching him from across the fire. He nodded as he looked from one to the other, noting that each of them seemed a little off. The dimensions of their faces were wrong. More space where there shouldn't be, less where there should be more.

They did not belong here.

"I know this world." He said and the men exchanged glances, nodding in agreement.

"Then you can help us," said the man to his right.

"How?"

"Guide us through this world."

"You want me to show you around?"

The man nodded and turned to look at one of the others. When he did Jamie noted the shape of his head. Instead of an oval it appeared more elongated, the jaw jutting from the bottom of the skull as if the mouth contained more teeth than there was room for. The thought sent a chill down his spine and he was afraid of what he was agreeing to do for these men.

"What are you looking for?" Jamie said.

"We seek the trinity."

"A trinity?"

All four nodded. "Three bound by a fourth. Our queen sent us to find the trinity before it forms."

"What happens then?" Jamie was struggling to come to grips with what they were talking about. Their words seemed off, yet he understood everything they were saying.

"Everything we know ceases to exist as darkness washes across the worlds. They do not understand the powers they have."

"Even this world?"

"Even this word will cease to exist."

"What then?" Jamie asked. He didn't care if this world died or not. They were kidding themselves to believe they could survive what happened. Maybe it would be best. What about Penny? What about her?

"What do you mean?"

"What happens after?"

At this the man shrugged, "no one knows, we've never faced the trinity before."

"Where are they?"

Again, the man shrugged. "We don't know. Some time ago Dravidic of the ivory court came across in search of the trinity, he's a wizard and knows things we do not. We believe if we follow him, he will lead us to them. The queen suspects he intends to use its power to take the throne for himself."

"Can you track him?"

"Of course, he lacks woodsman skills and doesn't know how to cover his trail."

"Then what do you need me for?" It was all becoming way too much to take in and a part of him suspected someone was trying to make a fool out of him. Ted, the name emerged. They were probably laughing at him right now.

"All right, what's the joke." Jamie pushed himself to his feet and walked around the campfire. "You can come out now, I know what you're up to," he shouted at the dark forest.

"A rough hand drove him to his seat. "Are you trying to get us killed. He could be out there right now watching us."

"Who?"

"Dravidic, or one of his familiars."

"You're serious."

"Of course."

"This is no joke?" The men stared at him across the fire, unmoved by his words, and it was then he realized each pair of eyes shone with a faint red glow.

"What are you?" He leaned forward.

"We are the Queens enforcers."

"What queen?"

"The alabaster queen. Have you not heard of her?"

"Can't say as I have."

One of the others nudged the speaker and said something in his ear. All Jamie could make out was a faint hissing that reminded him of the nest of rattlesnakes they'd cleaned out several years before on Bowers mountain.

"Not to worry, in time you will learn of the Queen and what she can do for you if you help."

"Which would be?"

"What would you like? Land, money, power, she can provide all of these things to those who help her cause."

"So, you're not from heaven?"

"What is this heaven you speak of."

"Some of my people believe it is where you go when you die, a land of milk and honey, its streets paved in god."

"That's odd, milk and honey can spoil, and gold is too soft to be used for a street."

"It's a belief not everyone holds."

"What do you believe?"

"I believe it's every man for himself. I believe being strong is better than being sorry."

"The queen would like a man such as you. Can you help us?"

"I'll help, can you do something for me."

"Name it."

"The place I come from is filled with bad people. They are holding my friend against her will. Can you help me free her?"

"We can, do we have a deal?" The man extended his hand.

"Of course." Jamie took the offered hand, noting the calluses on the man's thumb and palm. He didn't think they would figure out what was going on until it was too late, and by then he'd have what he wanted.

"By the way I'm Jamie, what's your name?"

They looked at one another with confused expressions.

Jamie patted chest with his open hand. "I'm Jamie."

The one across from him smiled and leaned back to pat his own chest. "I'm Balu."

"I'm Alme," the man on Balu's right said.

"They call me Etu," the man on Balu's left said.

"I am Lu," the last man said as he extended his hand and Jamie shook it. He felt like he'd just made a deal with the devil, and he knew all too well what happened to people who tried to trick an old trickster. He'd have to stay on his toes with these four, watch his back, and sleep with one eye open. If he got what he wanted, it would be worth it.

Alme Pushed himself to his feet and crossed to the deer where he retrieved the metal pot. Lifting it to his lips he slurped the contents then turned at him, his lips covered in dark red blood. He extended the pot to Jamie who struggled to keep from throwing up.

6

No moon hung in the night sky as Dravidic watched the enforcers camp from the top of a nearby ridge. He had no need of a fire, and even less of a need for company. He loved the night, embracing the security it offered, refuge from the light of reason.

As he watched over those who had been sent to find him he felt a presence. On his left a shadow emerged, towering over his diminutive figure as it came to stand next to him. They called them Wendigo, the flesh eaters of the forest. The Indians who once lived in these parts believed when one was touched by a Wendigo a hunger for human flesh was born. The hulking shape rocked impatiently from one foot to the other, its arms swinging back and forth, panting like a dog. Meaty hands brushed against the ground as it struggled to contain itself. The smell that preceded it spoke of the dead and dying, of things that have lain long beneath the surface of the ground. Its eyes offered the only light, a sickly yellow glow that would have sent Dravidic screaming over the edge into a sickening insanity, if he were a man.

Outwardly Dravidic looked like a man and carried himself as such. There was nothing to make you think otherwise save his eyes. If the eyes are the windows to the soul? What do they look into when no soul exists? Flat and lifeless, Dravidic's gaze was known to stop even the hardiest of men in their tracks. After all, how do you hurt someone who is not even alive?

Through the years he'd worn many faces and carried many different names. The one he sported now once belonged to a trader with a penchant for young female flesh. The trader's dalliances with a farmer's youngest daughter sealed his fate and when Dravidic, whose real name was lost to the ages, came upon him, he was hanging by the neck from a towering sycamore. The trader would not have been his first choice, but time had run out for him and he needed to make a quick exit, the Queen's enforcers were hot on his trail.

Dravidic, or the thing that wore his face, rubbed his neck with one gloved hand as a brief memory of the coarse rope filtered through his thoughts. The gloves he wore were of the finest kid leather taken from calves who'd only ever known the close confines of the crate where they were tethered to keep movement to a minimum. The material carried the memory of their misery and he breathed deeply of its scent, relishing their despair.

"Patience, my old friend," Dravidic said, reaching out to comfort the new arrival and still his rocking. "There will come a time when they are yours. Until then you need to watch over them, let no harm come to them until I say otherwise."

The groan was all the response he expected and needed, filled with bitter disappointment and an unholy need. Dravidic knew his word would be honored. The creatures of the night knew not to argue with him.

The figure vanished into the shadows, fading without a sound and Dravidic watched as it made its way across the valley that separated him from his pursuers. The dim lamps of its eyes guiding it as it silently moved through the emptiness. He would let them think they had him, and he'd play along until he grew bored with the game.

"Don't you ever get tired of playing your games." A young woman stepped out of the shadows behind Dravidic who smiled as he turned to confront her. She appeared as a slender young woman, yet her presence flickered briefly, revealing a gnarled old woman leaning upon a cane.

"And who are we playing this week Circe, or is it Grimhildr?"

"Don't you worry about it, and why are you here? I should tell Grimnahr."

Dravidic shrugged, he had no fear of man's pathetic little gods. "Do as you wish." He replied, his attention focused on the distant camp.

"What misery are you bringing us?"

"None at all, I bring hope for the future for all banished to the underworld. The Trinity will soon form and I'm here to take advantage of it and share the benefits of that power with my brethren."

"You're an old fool, no one can stop the trinity when the time comes."

"Who said anything about stopping it. My plan is to let it form."

"And seal our fates for another lifetime."

Dravidic smiled. "I have no time to argue with the likes of you. I have places to be, and things to do." With that he vanished into the shadows. It was a parlor trick as old as he. One he'd used many times to entertain a child queen when he was a sorcerer for the Ivory court.

Reality as most people knew it was similar to the pages of a book that lay one atop the other. For those who knew how, it was possible to slip behind the top layer, much like stepping behind the curtains on a stage and move unfettered across vast distances in a short period of time.

Dravidic appeared atop another ridge looking down upon a house that stood alone in shadowed depths. A single light burned in one of the windows. The house appeared to have been fortified to protect whoever lived there. It would do nicely, and he slipped back into the shadows to prepare for their coming.

7

Window sat with his back against the wall of the barn, hidden in the deep shadows cast by the light of the full moon riding across the starry sky. Without light pollution a million stars sparkled against the velvety blackness of the night. The cloudy band of the Milky Way cut a wide swath across the sky. A soft breeze was coming from the east, carrying with it the scent of fresh rain, and the stench of burning rubber. The faint cries of someone in distress faded in and out as the direction of the wind shifted.

He hated being alone, and with few exceptions, had found most of the survivors he knew to be tediously consumed with their own minor problems. Troubles that paled in comparison to the reality of the world in which they lived. With his pistol in his lap, the carved barrel rough against his fingers, he watched the night as it passed in a parade of shadows full of sinister intent.

His thoughts turned to the cabin in the woods and he was overwhelmed by helplessness as the old images blossomed. A simple table stood next to a fireplace where a roaring fire bathed everything in a yellow light. The smell of wood smoke competed with the stench of unwashed bodies. Four men sat around the table passing around a jar, each taking a drink as it came to them, their voices muted as they spoke in low rumbles that sounded like distant thunder. Their words indistinct, their features cast in shadows as they ignored his presence and concentrated on the contents of the jar.

Shuffling steps came from the black depths of the back room. Something moved in the emptiness and Window's stomach twisted in terror at the secrets that lay shrouded by the night.

The barn door opened beside him, pulling him from the memory, and he looked up as Meat stepped into the shadows. His arrival washed away the images that tried to intrude upon his solitude, saving him from the revelation he knew was coming as a face he recognized materialized from the emptiness. Her soft features had been twisted into the leer of a wild beast. Her glowing eyes boring into the deepest depths of his soul.

Window wiped his hand across his brow, trying to extinguish the recollection as Meat lowered himself to the ground next to him.

"Are you all right?"

"Yeah," Window said as the last of the memory faded into the nighted abyss of his past.

"Did Billie-Bob wake you in time?"

"Like clockwork, what is he always whispering about?"

"I don't know, I've never been able to catch what he's saying."

"That boys got some problems."

"And we don't. We've all seen things we shouldn't, done things we're not proud of, well everyone except Einstein."

"Is he gonna be all right?" Window asked.

"Who, Einstein?"

"Yeah, I don't think he's up to what we have to do."

"He'll be okay, I'm more concerned that I've gotten us involved in a wild goose chase. Who's to say those kids are even still alive. The sign is old and it's fading fast. If we don't catch up with them soon."

"They're only a couple of days ahead of us."

"Two days is a long time. What if there's more of them?"

"We'll handle it like we always have."

"I don't know, a part of me wants to keep going, bring those kids home, another part wants to go back, forget this whole thing, get on with my life," Meat said.

Window spotted movement from the corner of his eye. A lone figure watching them from the shaded depths of the forest bordering an overgrown field. The pale light of the full moon created pools of emptiness that threatened to envelope him. He looked back, searching for the figure, catching sight of a darker shadow as it shifted its position.

"Ssshhhh." Window placed his finger against his lips as he whispered, "there's something out there."

"Where?"

"In the tree line to the right of the old tractor." Window pointed and Meat squinted as he looked into the black depths beyond the abandoned tractor in the center of the field. A deeper shadow moved in the gloom.

"Do you think he can see us?"

"I don't know."

"Keep him in sight, I'm gonna slip around behind them."

"What if it's a zombie?" Window asked as Meat slipped out of his jacket and got to his feet.

"Then I'll kill it," Meat said before vanishing into the shadows.

Window watched his progress, what he could see of it. Meat had become one with the shadows. It wasn't long before he lost sight of him altogether and he shook his head as he shifted his position, making enough noise to keep whoever was watching interested.

Reacquiring the target, he settled back to watch, glancing to the right every so often as he searched for any sign of Meat. It was as if he'd become a ghost. Meat was going to have to teach him that trick.

8

Meat moved away from the barn, crouched low as he kept to the shadows. He made his way into the forest that surrounded the small farm. His skin crawling as he vanished into the gloom, the remnants of the nightmare that awakened him still fresh in his mind.

He'd been dreaming of that house again. An overgrown yard through which unseen things slithered in shadowed places. He and the man he called dad had taken refuge within silent walls that refused to be quiet. The whispered memories of the past lay at the indistinct edge of his consciousness, while the ghosts of a happier time moved through the rooms.

A swing set in the backyard offered mute testimony to the joy that once lived in the house. Its rusted chains creaking with a plaintive cry as an errant breeze stirred it. Photos on the mantle, covered in a thick layer of dust, proved this dead place once knew life, light, and the happiness of a growing family. In one photo, a man and woman stood together, the man's strong arms and their entwined hands resting on her swollen belly.

The photo frightened him. Filling him with sorrow for a child that might never know the joys life had to offer. Joys he'd never known. A part of him understood, with a maturity beyond his years, that his sorrow was as much for himself as it was for all the other children struggling to survive in a world turned upside down.

The sound of clawed feet scurrying about filled his mind as the memory of a solitary door at the end of a shadowed hallway emerged from the past. A brass knob glowed with a dull light and he reached for it as the cries of an infant, accompanied by frenzied squealing, came from beyond the faded façade.

He pushed the memory away as he slowed his steps to keep from stirring the dead leaves and alerting his target. He felt like he was straddling the past and the present as that memory refused to fade away. Carefully, he worked his way around until the tractor was directly between him and the barn. He knew then he was getting close and he stopped to listen.

From the shadows ahead came movement. Turning his head to the side, he watched from the corner of his eye. A trick he'd been taught by the man he called dad. He was rewarded with a glimpse of a shadowy form crouched at the tree line. The stranger was watching the barn and house alight with the ghostly glow of the full moon. They were unaware of Meat's presence.

He slowly eased around behind the watcher, maintaining his distance. The soft breeze stirring the leaves around them helped mask any sound he made. At the same time, it carried his scent away. He was approaching the figure when, warned of his approach by some primitive sixth sense, that shadowy form suddenly spun around to confront him. From the gloom came the sound of cold steel being drawn across leather and Meat spotted the faint glimmer of a blade.

"I'll cut ya," the figure hissed.

Meat stepped back, dodging the arc of the blade that narrowly missed laying open his throat. Stepping to the right, away from the blade, he lunged forward. His fingers struck flesh, but he failed to grab hold. The shadowy form dodged him and crouched low as it came in for a second attack.

Meat spun to the left, sidestepping the attack. As the figure passed, he grabbed an arm and yanked the person around, nearly losing his grip as the stranger cried out. He stepped in close, the scent of an unwashed body filling his nostrils, and wrapped his arm around a small neck. From the shadowy form came a strangled cry of surprise.

A small hand wrapped itself about Meat's wrist as the faint glimmer of the blade flashed in the shadows. The blade passed across his forearm with a sting of cold steel slicing through warm flesh. Meat slammed his fist it into the unseen face. The figure went limp as Meat held on, if he let go, he might lose the watcher in the depths of the gloomy forest around him.

Holding onto the stranger, Meat stepped out of the tree line into the overgrown field. In the pale light of the moon the stranger looked to be a boy, his torso bare, the flesh of his back and chest covered with black markings that made no sense. Meat looked up as Window crossed the field towards him.

"What did ya find?"

"Someone watching us. I don't know how long they've been there. We'll find out soon enough."

Window grabbed the young boy by his other arm and together they returned to the barn with their captive between them.

9

"Tie him up tight," Meat said as he and Window dropped their captive to the dirt floor of the barn. The boy was about ten years old, dressed in a loincloth fashioned from what appeared to be a set of curtains, the fabric was heavy and stiff, with a brocaded design in the filthy green cloth. His exposed flesh, while deeply tanned, was covered by crude tattoos, many of which were faded with time, attesting to their age.

Spirals and groups of jagged lines wrapped around his upper arms, and the flesh of both forearms was covered in odd swirling patterns that resembled pin striping. On each knuckle was a different letter that spelled out PAIN on one hand with LOVE on the other.

"Look at this," Window said as he rolled the boy over onto his back. His chest and stomach were covered by the tattoo of a man crucified on a cross and wrapped in barbed wire. Though crudely drawn, the shading of the image lent it a depth that made it appear to pop out of the boy's chest. The image hung down from between his nipples, the man's feet vanishing under the band of his loincloth. Above his left nipple was a Celtic trinity with a circle surrounding its central part.

Window grabbed a length of rope from one of the upright posts and quickly bound their captive's hands and feet, drawing them together behind his back.

The boy groaned as he regained consciousness. He fought against his bonds, yanking at the rope as he rolled over onto his side. Meat and Window stepped back as Einstein, rubbing the sleep from his eyes, came over to see what they'd found. Billie-Bob was still asleep in the back of the barn.

"Where did he come from?" Einstein said.

"I caught him spying on us," Meat said.

"Hey, you're bleeding." Window pointed at the blood on Meat's arm.

Meat examined the wound, it was superficial yet produced a good bit of blood, making it look worse than it really was.

"Grab me the first aid kit." Meat said, and Einstein nodded before he turned and rummaged through his pack where he'd been sleeping. He returned with a dirty white box he passed to Meat. With Window's help, he squirted a small amount of alcohol on the wound, gritting his teeth when the burning sensation hit him. The alcohol would kill any germs that might have gotten into the wound. Even a small cut like this was cause for worry. Without hospitals, or clinics, or even readily available doctors, a small wound could lead to death unless it was properly cared for.

Once Meat's arm had been taken care of, they turned their attention to the captive. The boy's eyes dripped hatred. "Cut me loose now or the master will feed you his pain. He'll eat your hearts out of you," he growled, exposing yellowed teeth that had been filed down to points.

Meat placed one booted foot on his chest as the boy strained against his bonds. He stretched his neck to bite Meat's foot, his teeth clicking together on empty air. It would be comical if not for the sheer rage that smoldered in his eyes.

"Shut up," Meat shouted, and slapped the boy across the face—hard—with his open hand.

"Fuck you," the boy screamed, spittle flying as he thrashed about on the dirt floor, stirring up clouds of dust.

Meat raised his fist and the boy stopped for a moment, glaring at Meat, daring him to hit him.

"I will eat your heart out of you," the boy hissed.

"Where are you from?" Meat said.

"Fuck you."

"What the hell is going on out here?" Gregory said, opening the door and entering the barn. "I heard shouting."

"We caught this one spying on us," Meat said, pointing at the young boy lying at his feet.

"He's a kid," Gregory said as he crossed to their captive. He stopped at the boy's figure, taking in the crude tattoos that covered his young body. "He's one of them."

"One of who?" Einstein said.

"One of the group that killed my wife and daughter. They were all dressed like this, like they were playing cowboys and Indians without the cowboys."

"Did you do that?" Meat said, prodding the young boy with the toe of his boot.

"Fuck you," the boy shouted, renewing his struggles to escape.

"Obviously that's the only word he knows," Window said as he drew his revolver and crossed to the boy. He squatted next to his supine figure and rested the long barrel of his pistol on his forearm. The boy settled down, mesmerized by the gun, his gaze softening as he traced the length of the barrel.

"What are you going to do?" Gregory said.

"What should have been done to begin with," Window said as he cocked his pistol and aimed the barrel at the boy's face.

The boy smiled, exposing pointed teeth, his eyes alight with what could only be characterized as joy. It appeared he understood the purpose of Window's pistol and was anxious to die. "Give me peace," he whispered as he strained to place his forehead against the muzzle.

"You can't do that, he's only a boy." Einstein pushed Window to the side and placed himself between their captive and the rest of them.

The boy screamed behind him, thrashing wildly, as he rolled around on the ground, struggling against his bonds.

"Get out of the way, Einstein."

"No."

"I'll shoot you first then." Window raised the muzzle of his pistol and aimed it at Einstein's head.

"Put the gun down," Meat said, placing his hand over Window's pistol and pushing it down.

Window sidestepped Meat and raised his pistol. "I always said you were weak. You don't have the stomach for what needs to be done."

"He's a kid," Einstein said. "This isn't like shooting a zombie. They're already dead so it doesn't matter."

"It was his kind that killed my wife and daughter," Gregory said, placing himself in Window's camp.

"How do you know it was him who did it? Maybe he's running with them for protection. Maybe he's a scared little kid like the rest of us," Einstein said.

"Speak for yourself," Window said.

"What's going on?" Billie-Bob emerged from the back of the barn wrapped in a blanket. He looked down at their captive. "Who's this?"

"We caught him spying on us." Window said.

Billie-Bob glanced at the crude tattoos that covered the boy's body as his face blanched and his eye widened. "They roared their terrible roars and gnashed their terrible teeth and rolled their terrible eyes and showed their terrible claws," he whispered before turning and retreating into the shadows at the back of the barn.

"What the hell was that all about?' Window said.

"I don't know." Meat was teetering on the edge of losing control over their small group. While there was never an official decision as to who would lead them, everyone assumed Meat would as he had the most experience outside the fence. It was a role that fit, and if they hoped to succeed, not to mention survive in the wilds, there had to be one person who was in charge.

There had to be control.

While he agreed with Window on what had to be done, he could understand Einstein's reluctance to carry through with it. They faced a dilemma that would pale in significance as they progressed through their quest. For now, it was a tough call, one he had to make if he was to cement his role as the leader.

They couldn't let the boy go. He'd only return to his group and warn his people, giving them time to prepare for their arrival.

If what they planned was to work, four against an unknown number, their arrival had to be a surprise. They couldn't leave him. He'd get loose and tell his tribe, or whatever it was he belonged to, about them, or he would die of exposure.

"We can't let him go," Meat said, stepping up and placing himself between Window and Einstein. He sensed the muzzle of Window's .44 aimed at the back of his head, and he hoped to hell no one caused Window to squeeze the hair trigger he knew it had. Of course, in that case, his problems would be solved.

"We can't kill him," Einstein said. "We'd be no better than them if we did."

"Then what do you want us to do?"

"I don't know."

"Do we leave him tied up in here?"

"We can't do that. How would he eat and drink? How would he get home?"

His comment silenced everyone. That was the crux of it. They all wanted to go home, not to Bremo Bluff. But to the time Gregory told them about the night before. Where a fast food joint could be found on every corner. Where you could walk the streets without fear of being attacked or eaten. Where you could lay down and go to sleep without fear of waking up as someone's prisoner, or worse.

"How about this, we leave him tied up with water close by so he can drink, and after we're done, on our way back through, we release him."

"What about food?"

Meat shook his head. "We only have enough for ourselves, and besides, it will only be a few days. I doubt he'll starve in that time."

"What about other animals coming to get him?"

"We'll keep the door locked from the outside so nothing can get to him."

As they debated his future, the young boy had worn himself out with his struggles. While Meat and Einstein reached an agreement they could live with, the boy had fallen asleep and was snoring, curled up as best he could into a ball on the dusty ground.

"Is that fair?" Meat said, turning to Window and Gregory. "We keep him prisoner until we return, then we let him go."

"Once he's out of the barn, he becomes fair game," Gregory said.

"What is wrong with you people?" Einstein said. "Whatever happened to compassion? To caring for those less fortunate than ourselves?"

"Have you been sleeping under a fucking rock or something?" Window said. "The world has changed, it's not like it was described in the books we've read. It's a dog eat dog world out there, and if you're not the biggest, baddest, son of a bitch out here, it'll eat you up."

"Like you?" Einstein said.

"Exactly like me," Window said as he moved closer to Einstein, invading his space, forcing him to take a step back.

"Let it go, we'll leave him in the barn until we come back through. After we release him, he's on his own. Now let's get ready to go. We've already fallen behind because of this." Meat turned away to pack his belongings for the coming day's hike.

Window and Einstein remained facing one another for a moment more, each refusing to be the first to step away, to concede to the other. Meat was quietly amused by Einstein's actions. He'd always been the quiet one, dutifully doing what needed done without complaint.

He did have a stubborn side to him, and Meat had seen him stand up to others before. Still he was concerned by what happened. There was nothing wrong with a bit of dissent in the ranks, as long as it didn't boil over into outright animosity. Right now, it looked like Einstein and Window had become mortal enemies, and he'd have to keep a close watch to make sure it didn't get out of hand.

Outside, the sky lightened as the sun emerged from the eastern horizon, greeted by the incessant chatter of the birds in the forest. Golden rays of light flowed across the steel roof of the barn where the struggle between life and death was being played out. Steam rose from the roof as the sun's rays heated the metal, offering a preview of the day's warmth.

They gathered in front of the barn preparing to head out when Gregory raced from his house with a backpack slung over one shoulder, his rifle over the other.

"Where are you going?"

"I want to come along, help out where I can."

"Can you use that thing?" Window said.

"I can hit anything inside eight hundred yards."

"That's good enough for me," Meat said.

"Wait a minute, I forgot something," Window said, and turned back to the barn. He vanished inside. From within came the roar of his pistol. Einstein screamed and raced back to the barn. Throwing open the doors to reveal Window standing over the body of their captor, the boy's blood staining the ground beneath his head.

"I did him a favor," Window said, slipping his pistol into the holster slung low on his hip.

Einstein screamed and charged Window, who sidestepped his attack. Einstein ran past his target, tripping over Window's extended foot, falling to the ground beside the body of their captive.

"Let it go," Meat shouted as Einstein pushed himself to his feet and prepared to charge again.

Gregory stepped between them, holding out his hands. "It's over," he said, "let it go."

Einstein dusted himself off and retrieved his gear from where he'd dropped it, glaring at Window who ignored him, as he casually walked to the group with a self-satisfied smile on his face.

"Why did you do that?" Meat said.

"It had to be done," Window said with a shrug.

"You'll get no argument from me, only we agreed to keep the boy captive until we returned, then we would let him go." Meat's control over the group was slipping through his fingers. If he didn't do something to establish order soon, they'd descend into anarchy.

What could he do? He had no experience with leadership. He knew if it got too far out of hand, the lives of the children counting on them would come to an end.

"Hey, Gregory," Billie-Bob said as he slung his rifle and stopped beside him, "do zombies eat popcorn with their fingers?"

"What? I don't know, what are you talking about? I guess."

Window and Meat turned away as Billie-Bob draped his arm over Gregory's shoulder.

"No, they save the fingers for last," Billie-Bob said. "Did you ever hear the one about the zombie that went to the whorehouse?"

Gregory shrugged.

"He wanted his money back because he couldn't get it up. He had DD, a dead dick." Billie-Bob finished with a guffaw. "Get it? Dead dick?" He slapped Gregory on the shoulder and bent over with laughter. "I've got a hundred of 'em."

Gregory shook his head as they trailed the rest of the group, Billie-Bob's voice running a mile a minute as he entertained his newfound audience.

10

Gregory had only one thing on his mind. Vengeance. Revenge for what the children did to his wife and daughter, payback for everything that had been taken from him since the dead walked. It was a mindset that ran counter to the way he was brought up. His parents were god fearing everyday folk who worked hard for all they had and tried to instill this beliefs in their children. For the most part he and his sister followed along. Attending church every Sunday, even after they moved out, praying regularly, and paying their tithe without complaint.

That all changed when the dead walked, and the beliefs instilled in them since an early age made them targets for those who would do them the most harm. After the awakening there was no room for turning the other cheek, no room for forgiveness. It became a dog eat dog world they were ill prepared to survive in. Everything they'd been taught was turned upon its head. None of them were ready physically, or mentally for the brutality washing across the world.

Vengeance is mine; I will repay, saith the lord.

No. He decided. *Vengeance will be mine.*

The boys he accompanied seemed better suited to this new world. More adept at surviving, ready to meet the worlds brutality on its own terms. Meat, Window, and Einstein walked ahead of him. In a staggered formation on both sides of the track. Towering black clouds dominated the sky beyond, turning the day to evening as they followed the rusted rails. Here and there saplings had pushed through the roadbed, their narrow trunks bending to a steady breeze blowing from the east.

He glanced back at Billie-Bob who walked the rail like a tightrope. He carried himself with a predatory grace and a part of Gregory felt a note of sorrow at the loss of the boy's innocence. All they'd known was the brutality of a world that moved on from caring. The innocence of their childhood lost to despair.

He noted how Billie-Bob whispered to himself, as if he were chanting, and Gregory slowed his steps to catch what he was saying. It was at that moment he felt it. Rising through his feet, a faint rumble that came from the roadbed.

He'd felt it before, as a child, when he and his friends would watch the three fifteen as it wound its way along the rails, pulling a long line of empty coal cars behind it. Later that night another train would come through with fully loaded coal cars destined for the port in Hampton Roads.

The air around him became charged with static electricity, the scent of ozone heavy on his tongue. Every hair on his body felt like it was standing on end. Billie-Bob felt it as well for he stopped and turned to face the way they'd come.

Brief flashes of blue lightning danced along the rails as a gust of wind shrieked with a mournful voice. Gregory staggered back against this unexpected blast. The screeching of metal against metal filled the day. Sparks flew as a powerful light threw Billie-bob into silhouette, nearly blinding Gregory. The ear shattering shriek of an air horn split the day. The boy stood rooted in place, transfixed by the train bearing down on him, a deer caught in the headlights of an approaching car.

All Roads Lead to Terror

Gregory screamed a warning and pushed Billie-Bob off the rail, both of them crashing to the roadbed as the wind from the passing train snatched at them with greedy fingers. Gregory rolled over and pushed himself to his feet, struck speechless by the sudden appearance of the Amtrak.

Where did it come from? No train had ridden these rails in more than a decade. Now an Amtrak was passing through.

Gregory watched as it rumbled by, softly lit windows offered brief glimpse of the passengers inside. Many were reading newspapers, some gazed unseeing out the window. One in particular caught his attention. A young boy standing on a seat at the window, his hands cupped around his face as he watched their passing figures. He recognized the child, and that recognition dredged up a memory from the past.

It had been a good year. He and his sister had excelled in their studies, passing with flying colors, and as a reward for their hard work their parents planned a day trip to Richmond. At the time Amtrak offered weekend connections between Charlottesville and Richmond. Gregory was more excited about the train ride and spent nearly the entire time watching the passing scenery. He clearly remembered seeing an armed man and a boy along the tracks and brought this to his father's attention only to be told not to worry about it.

At the time he forgot about it, now as he looked back, he began to question what he'd seen. It wasn't possible for two moments in time, separated by thirty plus years, to converge out here in the middle of nowhere. It was a coincidence that made little sense unless larger forces were at play. He once believed in God, so it wasn't a stretch of the imagination to believe something else existed beyond their understanding.

"Where the hell did that come from?" Billie-Bob dusted himself off. The other three ran back to where they stood while Gregory searched for any sign of the train. It was like it had fallen off the end of the world, vanishing into the gloom of the overcast day.

"What was that?" Window said, joining them as Einstein and Meat followed.

"Where did it come from?" Meat said.

"The bigger question is where did it go?" Einstein knelt at the rail and ran his hand over its rusty surface. "Still cold, never been touched." He pushed himself to his feet, his gaze drifting in the same direction as the others, down the rails, in the direction the train vanished.

"Anybody know what just happened?" Meat looked from one to the other, each of them shaking their head.

Gregory suspected he might know the answer, but he kept his mouth shut. He wasn't even sure his answer was the right one. In his freshman year at college, he and several of his friends became interested in the paranormal. Like other colleges with a history reaching back for more than a hundred years, the grounds and several buildings at the University of Virginia campus in Charlottesville were known to be haunted. The writer many viewed as the master of horror, Edgar Allen Poe, once studied there. It was suspected the local ghost stories served as inspiration for his dark writings.

While they were never confronted by any of the ghosts they sought, there were several instances when they felt like they were in the presence of something beyond their understanding. Parts of certain rooms remained ice cold while the rest of campus sweltered in the August heat. Odd sounds in the middle of the night, or soft voices offering whispered warnings from beyond the grave.

Chelsea, the only girl in their group, claimed to have felt an icy hand on her shoulder during one of their nocturnal visits to the Alderman library, where Doctor Green's personal book collection resided. He'd been a confederate surgeon during the civil war and there'd been several reported sightings of his ghost dusting the books. After that Chelsea refused to join them, and left school at the end of the semester. Last he heard she dropped out of school entirely.

"A blast from the past," Einstein said. "a ghost maybe?"

"Was it really there?" Billie-Bob said.

"We all saw it, didn't we?" Meat said.

Window, who'd remained silent throughout, stepped into the middle of the tracks. "Whatever it was, it's gone now, and we need to keep going.

Each in turn nodded as a chill washed across Gregory's arms. Something else was going on behind the scenes. Something he couldn't put his finger on in any rational way. There was no such thing as a coincidence, everything happened for a reason. Were these four boys' part of a bigger picture?

Or was he putting too much into a random occurrence?

11

Reaching the outskirts of the small town of Columbia, Meat called a halt and they gathered on a slight rise overlooking the town. Route six ran through the middle of Columbia, no more than a scattering of houses gathered around two churches, and an old train station. A bronze plaque in front noted that the building was listed on the register of historic places by the National Historical Society.

The society no longer existed, all of its members were dead. Their mission to preserve what survived the wrecking ball in man's pursuit of progress had been unable to survive man's own inhumanity to man.

A dense layer of *a mile a minute vine*, a trailing vine that grew faster than it could be cut, covered practically everything. Across from the station stood a group of houses gathered around two old churches. One of the spires had fallen, the result of high winds, vandalism, and neglect. Or a combination of all three.

The contents of one house covered its front lawn, the furnishings no more than humps beneath a sea of the ever present *a mile a minute* that threatened to consume the house itself.

"Why do zombies eat brains with their fingers?" Billie-Bob said.

"I thought they saved the fingers for last?" Gregory answered with a shrug.

Billie-Bob struggled to restrain a giggle, "they're not coordinated enough to use utensils." He finished with a guffaw as he slapped his thigh with his hand. "Do you get it? They don't know how to use a fork."

Gregory smiled as Billie-Bob resumed his whispered monologue, speaking in a soft voice, the words coming at a staccato, rapid-fire rate. "They roared their terrible roars and gnashed their terrible teeth and rolled their terrible eyes and showed their terrible claws," He chanted, repeating the phrase over and over again like a mantra to protect him.

"Is he always like this?" Gregory pointed at Billie-Bob with his thumb.

"Every day." Window smiled.

Along the right shoulder, close to route six, stood a two-story house that looked like it once held a business. From the railing of the balcony on the second floor hung three corpses.

Beneath each body lay a grisly pile of bones with some connecting tissue still intact. Each had been shot in the head, ensuring that they wouldn't return for revenge, the blood splatter on the once white wall of the building behind them had faded to a dirty brown color.

Was that one of the missing crews? Meat wondered as he walked by. Scavenging crews had managed to explore all the points of the compass surrounding Bremo Bluff with the exception of the land to the east. So far, three crews had vanished without a trace in the wilds between the Bluffs and the Atlantic Ocean.

When Meat first approached the council about going after the children, they'd been reluctant to give their blessing, content to mark them off as lost for good. Yet, at the same time, they had to learn what lay to the east, and whether it posed a threat to the compound. A point Meat used to hammer at their reluctance until they relented, with one caveat. A stipulation that even in the present seemed overly brutal to Meat.

There would be no survivors.

At first, he balked at the requirement. Killing those who had taken the children would make them no better than the people they pursued, or the roving bands of survivors who took what they wanted, killing anyone who got in their way. Yet, he understood their reasoning, and with reluctance he accepted their terms.

He had not yet shared this stipulation with the others. After all, what happened beyond the fence, stayed beyond the fence. If they chose not to carry through with the council's wishes, would they know?

As a group, they silently walked past the building. Even Billie-Bob had grown quiet as the hollow sound of their footsteps echoed from the stillness around them. As they each passed, they glanced in the direction of the hanging corpses then cast their eyes down at their feet.

This was real.

They'd all seen zombies in the past. Had shot at them as they gathered beyond the fence at Bremo Bluff. A fence that protected them from the reality of what they faced, keeping them safe in the security of the community.

Out here, away from the fence, their safety lay in their numbers, and an ever-watchful nature nurtured by a childhood spoiled by events beyond their control. They were the children of the apocalypse, survivors hardened by an ever-present death that was no longer hidden from view. Since that fateful day in March, death had become the norm, an acceptable alternative to what waited all of them in their final moments.

Moving beyond Columbia, they entered a wilderness bisected by the crumbling pavement of route six. Mother Nature had nearly reclaimed what man had taken. Saplings grew from the center of the macadam, their roots cracking the once smooth surface, permitting small brush to emerge. Here and there, bare spots of weathered asphalt offered the only evidence of the once busy throughway that connected Western Virginia with Richmond.

The rusting hulks of automobiles sat haphazardly where they had been abandoned. The ever present *a mile a minute* consuming them as weeds grew from their exposed interiors. They dotted the cracked macadam, their shadowy depths offering refuge to a varied assortment of small animals.

Above them the sky had grown darker as a cool breeze stirred the leaves of the forest, speaking to them in its secret voice as the scent of rain came carried upon its currents. Another scent mingled with that of the rain, a darker odor, an earthy fragrance that spoke of things long dead.

"We're going to have to find shelter for the night," Meat said.

"Why don't we go back to Columbia?" Einstein said.

Meat shook his head as a gust of wind threatened to strip his hat from his head. "I want to keep pushing forward. We'll find something."

"I hope you're right."

With their heads bent to the wind, they pushed into the approaching storm as it kicked up around them. Fat raindrops fell from the dark sky as lightning danced in the distance, its booming voice trailing a few seconds behind. The leaves of the trees around them turned their backs to the wind, a sign this would be a bad one.

Lightning streaked across the sky above their heads, filling the air with an electric tang as the crackling sound of thunder shook them to the marrow of their bones. The deluge had yet to start, it wouldn't be long, and Meat scanned the forest ahead for any sign of shelter.

Maybe he should have let them turn back?

Then he spotted it, screened by trees on the left side of the road—a ranch style house sitting back from the highway, nearly hidden behind a front yard slowly being reclaimed by the forest around it.

"Up ahead," he shouted as the frequency of the falling raindrops intensified. They ran to the house, across the lawn where small trees sprouted, and to the front door where they gathered under the narrow roof that afforded some protection from the storm. Meat forced the door open and it swung into the shadowy depths of the house as the musty scent of decay greeted them.

12

They fanned out across the small living room, carefully checking each room of the house until they confirmed the house was empty. In the back they found the kitchen, and against the back wall of the screened-in porch sat an old wood fired cook stove that still worked.

Someone had used the stove recently. Ashes filled the firebox. On the flat surface sat a cast iron skillet, its bottom coated by a layer of grease.

Meat sniffed the pan, noting the grease was still relatively fresh, and as his eyes scanned the small kitchen, he picked out signs that someone was using it as a shelter. Maybe they had been passing through and wouldn't return to find they them invading their space.

He hoped so.

Situations like this one tended to spiral out of control with gunplay entering the equation more often than not. It had become easier to shoot your problem, than deal with it in a rational manner. Compromise had given way to a Wild West attitude.

In no time, they had built a small fire that provided warmth and heat for cooking. In the cast iron skillet they prepared a feast of venison stew from the deer jerky they carried, boiling it down as best they could in rainwater, adding potatoes and carrots from the garden they maintained year round, along with several spring onions they'd picked up along the way.

Their bellies full, they sat around the stove as night descended and the rain continued to tap against the roof in a steady rhythm that lulled them into a false sense of security. Failing to post a guard, they nodded off to sleep.

Einstein was the first to stir. It had become colder, and he awakened to find the fire out. While starting another, the rest of the group sleeping around him, the sound of movement came from beneath his feet. Window stirred on his right as Einstein turned his ear to the house, straining to find out more.

A distinct thump came from below them.

"What's that?" Window sat up, looking around as he rubbed the sleep from his eyes. "Who's on guard?"

"Ssshhh." Einstein put his finger to his lips to quiet him. To Window's right, Meat and Billie-Bob slept, breathing in the steady rhythm of deep sleep. Beyond them, curled up next to the wall, lost in dreams of what had once been, Gregory lay wrapped in a dirty blanket.

The thump came again, and Window pushed himself up from his seat. He leaned over to wake Meat. Einstein stopped him. "It's probably nothing. I'll go check it out."

"I'll come with you." Window strapped on his holster and checked the chambers of his revolver.

Lighting a candle from the fire he'd started, Einstein led the way, holding the candle high, his hand cupped to protect the flame as they crossed the kitchen. The sound of movement came from beneath their feet.

"It's in the basement." Einstein reached a door and opened it to reveal a small pantry, its shelves bare. Moving to the next door, he opened it to reveal a yawning black pit. From the inky well of darkness came the sound of movement and Einstein knelt down on the top step to shed some light into the basement. At the very edge of that faint pool of illumination a couch sat against the wall of the finished basement.

Einstein carefully moved down the steps with Window close behind. He might still be upset over what Window had done. At the time, as they descended into darkness, Einstein was happy Window backed him up.

Reaching the bottom, the faint glow of the candle illuminated the entire room. Two easy chairs occupied the wall next to the couch. Across from it stood a massive flat panel television, and on the rack next to it sat several pieces of recording equipment along with two game consoles. A thick layer of dust covered everything, and the wires connecting it all together had been chewed clean through, leaving nubs protruding from the rear of the components.

To the left of the easy chairs, a narrow hallway vanished into the emptiness crowded around the small pool of light given off by the candle. The sound of movement came from those black depths and Einstein glanced at Window with a worried expression.

"What's wrong?" Window said.

"I don't think I want to go in there."

"I'm right behind you."

"That's what worries me."

"Go on, you've brought us this far, we might as well finish."

"You're right." Einstein turned back to the hallway. As he moved forward, the leading edge of the faint pool of light illuminated the floor. Inside the hallway, the light exposed a pair bare feet, the nails cracked and jagged, the flesh gray with death.

Einstein stopped, his heart climbing into his throat as he lifted the candle higher to expose more of the person standing there. He spotted the hem of a dress, filthy and torn, the front stained with a large swath of dried blood that appeared black in the candlelight.

She lurched forward, drawn by the light, her hands stretched out as she stumbled forward. With a moan of fear, Einstein stumbled back into Window, knocking him back against the couch, forcing Window to sit down as Einstein plopped down beside him.

"Shoot her, dammit," Einstein shouted.

Window clawed his pistol from its holster and lifted the muzzle, aiming at the woman's head.

"Shoot her," Einstein screamed as he struggled to back away from the woman, clawing his way up the back of the sofa, the flame of the candle fluttering in response to his movement, sending shadows dancing across the walls as shouts and pounding footsteps came from the stairs. Einstein's yell had awakened the others.

Window sat unmoving, the pistol forgotten in his hand, his eyes fixed on the woman's face as a single word formed on his lips.

"Mom."

13

Drops of rain clung to the window before Meat, chilling the glass and forming a frame of condensation around the perimeter of each pane. In the sky beyond dark clouds churned violently, crowded low to the ground, as rain pelted the roof above his head with a steady drone. He knew this place, had learned to read within its walls. The classroom at Bremo Bluff.

What am I doing here?

The classroom was empty, and he and Anna worked to clean up. It seemed odd that he had been assigned to help in the school instead of with one of the scavenging crews on their varied searches beyond the fence. He wasn't complaining.

Along with the warmth he had the added pleasure of working with Anna, who caught his eye several weeks earlier, emerging from her bulky winter clothing like a butterfly after a long harsh winter. Working inside with her sure beat working in the cold rain. The warmth enveloped him in a comforting embrace that lulled him into a sense of security he'd never known. So warm that Anna wore only a pair of shorts and a halter-top.

A faint yell intruded upon the scene, coming from the darkened hallway beyond the door of the classroom. Meat glanced in that direction as a cold chill whispered down his spine.

Maybe I should help them.

Anna crossed the room, touching his arm as she stood within the arc of his legs splayed out before him, one bare thigh resting gently against his own. Even though he wore pants, the sensation of her flesh against his was electrifying, sending jolts of delicious anticipation coursing through his body, deepening that feeling of secure warmth that enveloped him. Carnal images whispered through his mind as he hesitantly reached out to touch one of her breasts wrapped in the thin fabric of the halter-top.

The scream came again, filled with terror, a man crying out for aid. He glanced at the door where he spotted Window watching them through the crack in the door that stood ajar. "You said you would help."

Meat returned his attention to Anna, who stood naked before. "It's so hot in here." She fanned her face with her hand. "Wouldn't you feel more comfortable without all these clothes?"

He didn't question the how or why of what was happening, buoyed upon a volatile sea of yearning. Meat nodded as he tried to look at her secret place, shrouded in shadows his gaze could not penetrate. He'd seen naked women before while growing up, some dead, some alive, and others stuck in the hell in between. None of them made him feel the way Anna did.

The sound of something slapping against the glass came from the row of windows along the wall on his left. A horde of zombies gathered there, slapping against the glass with melting flesh. Blood smeared its surface, the rain washing it away in some places. The image overwhelmed his desire, leaving him cold and lifeless inside.

"Don't you love me anymore?" Anna asked, her voice low, grating, a guttural sound that came from deep in her throat.

She had changed. Her once soft flesh was hard and gray, mottled with black spots where decay was advancing. She grasped his head in her hands, her cracked nails raking the flesh of his cheeks. She opened her mouth as she leaned forward, rotting teeth like the slats of a fence behind her twisted lips. He pushed her away with his foot.

"Shoot her," Einstein yelled, his voice coming from some distance away. "Shoot her," Einstein screamed, his shout driving away the dream. Meat opened his eyes on a dark world.

For a moment disorientation overwhelmed him. The memory of finding the old house filtered through his mind, mingling with the memory of another old house that lay shrouded by shadowed wisps of terror that sent his heart racing as it squeezed his windpipe in a chilled grasp. He sat up, glancing at Billie-Bob and Gregory who lay to his right, sleeping. From his left came the sound of a struggle.

"Shoot her, dammit," Einstein shouted from somewhere in the depths of the house, and Meat jumped to his feet. Though a fire burned in the stove, a chill caressed his flesh, the night sky beyond the kitchen window alight with a full moon partially hidden behind dense clouds that carried the promise of rain.

Crossing the kitchen, he came to the open basement door, and in the shadowy depths below, spotted the light of a candle that illuminated the end of a couch where Einstein sat. Only he wasn't sitting. He had crawled halfway up the back, struggling with something beyond Meat's view.

Meat took the steps two at a time, his pistol in his hand as he entered the finished basement to find Einstein struggling with an older woman who had turned. He drew a bead on the side of the woman's head, a part of him wondering why Window sat there, his gun in his hand, staring at the woman with rapt attention.

The sound of the shot was deafening in the confines of the basement, that violent roar amplified by the close walls, to leave a ringing in his ears. The round hit the woman in the side of the head, high and to the right, a spray of blood marking its entry point. The soft nosed bullet expanded as it penetrated her skull, shattering bone, and slicing off the top of her skull that landed on the floor at Window's feet. Instead of dropping instantly, she folded up slowly, her knees buckling as her motor controls quit functioning, and she rolled backwards onto the floor to gaze unseeing at the ceiling as the last of her bastardized life drained away.

"What the fuck's wrong with you?" Einstein shouted as he turned to confront Window, his voice tight with emotion. "Why didn't you shoot her?"

Window turned his head slowly, looking up at Einstein with a faraway expression in his eyes, as if he wasn't really there.

Footsteps sounded from above as Gregory, followed by Billie-Bob, crowded down the steps.

"What happened?" Gregory spotted the dead zombie lying on the floor at Window's feet.

"I heard a noise in the basement," Einstein said. "We came down to find out what it was, and she attacked us."

"And Window killed her," Billie-Bob said.

Einstein shook his head and pointed at Meat as he pushed himself off the couch to stand on shaking legs. Window remained in his seat. His gaze fixed on the corpse at his feet.

Gregory crossed to the corpse and knelt alongside it. "It hasn't been that long since she turned. There might be others."

"Are there anymore?" Meat crossed to the darkened hallway and peered down its shadowy length.

"I think she's the only one," Einstein said. "Why didn't you shoot her?" He swiveled his head to look at Window. "Are you trying to get me killed?"

"We better check the rest of the basement." Meat turned back to the hallway. Einstein and Gregory followed as Billie-Bob remained with Window, who had yet to move from the couch.

Three doors greeted them as they moved into the hallway, one on the right, another opposite, and one at the end. All three closed. At the first door, Meat turned the knob and pushed it open slowly. Einstein entered behind him and held up the candle so they could see what lay beyond. The stench of a sewer greeted them as the door opened upon a small bathroom. The toilet had not been flushed in a long time.

Stepping back, he closed the door firmly before turning to the door opposite. In that room they found a bed covered with blankets and clothing. The filthy sheets looked like they had been used recently., They carried the sour scent of an unwashed body. A pile of dirty clothes sat against the opposite wall. The closet door stood open, empty, a lonely wire clothes hanger on the closet rod.

Back in the hallway, they cautiously approached the last room. If any more zombies remained, they'd be hidden behind this one. The surface had been marred by what looked like bloody smears. Taking a deep breath, Meat turned the knob and leaned into the door, pushing it open. In this room stood another bed with a nest of clothes and blankets, more dirty clothes piled against the far wall. Like the other room, all of the clothes belonged to a woman.

As he turned to leave, the unmistakable sound of someone moaning came from beneath the pile. Stepping back into the room, he rounded the bed, the muzzle of his pistol aimed at the floor as he approached the pile of clothes. He probed them with his foot, coming into contact with something hard. He kicked aside the clothes to uncover a person crouching on their hands and knees, their long hair hanging to the floor as they shook with fear.

"It's okay." Meat knelt. "I'm not going to hurt you."

She was a young girl, fourteen, possibly fifteen years old, and she lifted her head to look at him with terror-filled eyes. Her face was dirty, her eyes haunted as they darted left and right.

"Sssssssshhhhh," she said, holding a finger to her lips.

"It's okay, you're safe now," Meat said.

She shook her head as she looked over Meat's shoulder. "She's out there waiting for me."

Meat shook his head. "Who's out there?"

"Mom." The girl's eyes widened with remembered terror. "She kept trying to get in, but I wouldn't let her."

"What happened to her?" Meat said, trying to keep her talking until he could get her to come out.

"She tripped down the steps in the dark. I think she broke her neck."

"Is there anybody else here?"

"Daddy left a long time ago. He went to get water and never came back. Jamie died last year but wouldn't stay in the ground. He kept digging himself out and coming to the back door, pounding on it for us to let him in." She clamped her hands over her ears as she relived the memory.

"He's gone," Meat said. "Take my hand, it's safe." He held out his hand for her.

She reached out hesitantly as her brow furrowed, "Are you real?"

Meat smiled. "I certainly hope so."

As her hand met his, an electric spark of desire raced the length of his arm. It reminded him of his recently vacated dream.

All Roads Lead to Terror

Beneath all the grime and dirty clothes, she was a girl, and Meat's hormones surged in response to her proximity as that new, yet familiar stirring came from his loins. The purple-headed bastard woke up and as he stood up, he quickly adjusted himself to make room. It didn't feel right referring to it by that name, yet his limited experience with the opposite sex forced him to fall back upon familiar schoolyard jargon.

The adults tried to teach them about sex and babies, unfortunately the greater needs of survival offered little time for such things. It was a natural process, and the adults were confident that each of them would in time figure things out, as it had been done since the day of the caveman.

Maria's proximity made Meat aware of how filthy they all were. Water's scarcity in this new age had caused a monumental shift in thinking towards personal hygiene. While they could make drinking water in the Bluffs, it had to be rationed to make sure everyone got their share.

The outlet lines of the steam turbines at the power plant offered a nearly limitless supply of hot clean water, and the proximity of the river permitted many of the inhabitants to bathe regularly. The one thing that hadn't changed with the awakening was an adolescent's disdain for bathing. The only difference now, no one was riding them to get a bath every day.

She stood unsteadily on her feet. The flickering light of the candle threw shadows onto the walls around them. She jerked her head left and right, trying to catch a glimpse of whatever lurked in her peripheral vision. She smiled, revealing a row of fairly straight, yet dirty teeth that to Meat was like a ray of sunshine suddenly breaking through an overcast day.

"Who do we have here?" Gregory said as Meat led the girl across the room. He realized he'd never asked her name.

"I'm Maria." She followed Meat into the hallway where Einstein and Billie-Bob waited. They stepped back as Meat led her into the family room where Window sat on the couch, the dead woman at his feet.

"Mom." Maria crossed to the woman and dropped to her knees as tears rolled down her cheeks. She ran her hand along her mother's cheek, her other hand covering her mouth as she bent her head and cried silently.

Meat crossed to Window and knelt next to him, placing his hand on the boy's knee as he looked into his eyes. What he found frightened him. Window had always been the strong, quiet one in the group. A quality Meat had grown accustomed to and came to count on. A sense of loss filled him when he realized Window wasn't really with them. He might have been physically sitting on the couch, yet mentally he'd become lost in his memories.

Meat glanced at the dead woman. Maria bent over and gently kissed her mother's cheek, then wiping her eyes, she pushed herself to her feet.

"Is he all right?" she said, motioning to Window.

"I think so. Come on, Window, let's go upstairs." Meat stood up and took Window's hand. Window followed willingly enough, and as the first light of a new dawn filled the cloudy sky, they gathered in the kitchen.

14

Meat and the others gathered around the wood stove as they dined on cans of Spam Maria retrieved from the basement. Their good by date had passed a number of years ago, of course everything else was outdated in the world. They'd been stored in a cool dry place, so they stood little chance of getting sick. Over time, their bodies had adapted to the changes forced upon them, making outdated food less of a danger than it might have been, and a welcome change from the steady diet of rabbit, squirrel, and deer.

"So where are you guys from?" Maria said.

"A place down the road, past the bend in the river, you know, on the right," Billie-Bob said, drawing a look from Meat that warned him to be careful. "I'm not telling her anything important."

"What's wrong?" Maria glanced from Billie-Bob to Meat, then back again with a worried expression.

"They're all a bunch of old ladies where we come from, always afraid someone will find them. They're as bad as my brother," Billie-Bob said.

"You have a brother? What's his name? Is he older? Younger? I'm sorry, I haven't had anyone to talk to in so long."

"His name's Bobbie, and he's the same age as me."

A confused look crossed Maria's face. "And you're Billie-Bob, right?"

"Billie. They call me Billie-Bob because me and my brother are twins, and while growing up, we'd trade places to confuse people. Everyone calls us both Billie-Bob now."

"It sounds so confusing."

"How long has your dad been gone?" Meat said.

"He left a year or so ago, I think. I'm not sure, we've been hiding here for so long. I'm sorry, I didn't catch your name."

He extended his hand, hoping to once again hold hers. "They call me Meat."

"Why such an odd name? I'm sorry, I didn't mean to offend you."

"It's all right."

"It was only you and your mom?" Gregory said.

"Since last year, I think. Jamie, he was my younger brother, he came down with a fever and died. We buried him…" Her emotions overwhelmed her. Billie-Bob placed his hand on her back, and she turned in her seat to bury her face against his shoulder.

Her actions sparked a touch of jealousy in Meat who sat on her other side. Everyone became quiet as Maria fought to get her emotions under control. Window had been quiet throughout, eating when Meat instructed him to do so, a part of the group in only a physical sense. Like he was off in a world all his own.

Meat noticed Einstein watching Window.

He knew what was wrong and needed to get it out in the open as soon as possible if they hoped to be successful, much less survive what they intended to do. It wouldn't do them any good as a group to have two of their members angry at one another. Next was the question of Maria and what to do with her. He didn't really want her to come along. Not with what they planned to do. He'd only allowed Gregory to accompany them because he had lost his wife and daughter to that band of savages. His motive for coming along was very obvious. He wanted revenge.

All Roads Lead to Terror

There would be no survivors who could reveal the location of Bremo Bluff. It was a matter of survival and the presence of the group, especially since they knew what lay at Bremo Bluff, meant they would have to be destroyed.

"Is anything wrong?" Meat said.

"More than you realize." Einstein's gaze drifted over to Meat. His brow was wrinkled in anger, reminding Meat of their first meeting in class when Einstein was eight. It was during recess and Einstein had been cornered by two of the larger boys in class. Even after an apocalypse, some things never changed—bullies would always go after those they perceived as being weaker, though in this new reality, weakness was sometimes characterized by an unwillingness to do what was necessary to survive.

They had been learning to raise rabbits. The three R's—reading, writing and arithmetic—had been replaced in this new reality by resource, raise, and re-purpose. Rabbit meat was good and with the animal's ability to reproduce, it had become a staple of the community. They had reached the last lesson, harvesting, and the instructor had shown them how to quickly and efficiently break the rabbit's neck to minimize its suffering.

It was at this point Einstein hesitated, having become attached to his charges; he was unable to bring himself to kill the animals he'd spent the past months caring for. The two biggest boys in the group had no problem with harvesting and quickly dispatched their own small herds before moving among their classmates dispatching what the others hesitated to kill. When they came to Einstein, he tried to stop them, his actions angering the boys, who took a great deal of pleasure in the suffering of Einstein's animal, dragging out its death as the rabbit screamed in agony.

A rabbit's scream is something that stays with a person, a cry reminiscent of a baby's squall. A chilling sound that stirred old memories better left undisturbed as the image of that lone door at the end of a shadowy hallway invaded Meat's mind.

Einstein had thrown himself at his tormentors in a flurry of fists as ineffective as his ability to do what was needed to survive. The teacher intervened, an old man who had less patience for Einstein's feelings than for those of the rabbits he'd been teaching them to raise.

Meat and Window had been hanging out together since Window's arrival. Gravitating to one another, two lost souls looking for something neither of them could explain rationally. Their paths to the Bluffs, while similar, had been as different as night and day. Two years older than Einstein, they'd already taken the class for raising rabbits and currently oversaw several small herds they'd started from the wild rabbits they captured beyond the fence. In the small school yard, they came upon Einstein cornered by his tormentors. His ferocity in the face of such odds impressed even Window.

Einstein refused to give up. With a busted lip, one eye nearly swollen closed, and blood from his nose smearing the front of his shirt, he stood his ground. Holding his fists up in an attempt to defend himself as they pummeled him at their leisure.

"Don't seem fair two against one." Window came up behind them.

"This ain't none of your business, Window," Franklin, the oldest, said. His father was currently serving on the council and from the way Franklin acted, you'd think it was he who was serving. The fact that his family had been among the founders of this outpost further added to his sense of entitlement.

"I'm making it my business," Window said.

"I don't need no help," Einstein said through tears of anger and frustration.

"Could have fooled me."

Franklin and his friend turned their attention from Einstein to Window, two big boys who felt confident they had the upper hand. Meat caught the look in Window's eyes, a wild glee, a barely restrained rage that flashed in greedy anticipation. Faster than they could react, Window drove into Franklin's friend, hyper extending his knee with a well-placed kick right beneath the kneecap, followed up with a one two combination that doubled him over and set him up for a crushing uppercut that sent him falling to the ground like a tree felled in the forest.

It happened so fast Franklin barely had time to react. One moment he and his friend towered over what they considered easy pickings. In the next his friend was lying at his feet unconscious while Window stood silently in front of him, his hands on his hips as he gazed at him with eyes that carried a quiet contempt.

Franklin held up his hands as he backed away from Window. "I don't want no part of this," he said.

"That should even things up." Window turned on the ball of one foot and walked away.

With a smile, Einstein advanced on Franklin, who once he was alone, realized how vulnerable he was.

The memory receded as Meat once more came face to face with the problem that was growing within their ranks. Twice now Window and Einstein had clashed over differences. At the barn,

Window had been right, and Einstein was wrong. Now there appeared to be a new problem.

"It's like he's trying to get me killed," Einstein said.

Window jumped to his feet and walked to the back door. His gaze fixed on the forest behind the house.

"What's wrong?" Maria said, looking up from Billie-Bob's shoulder as Window brushed past her.

Window pushed through the back door and raced down the steps into the backyard. He ran across the yard, vanishing into the forest behind the house.

15

Meat followed, stopping at the door long enough to tell everyone else to stay put. He ran out into the rain and followed Window who was weaving among the trees of the forest. After fifteen minutes, Window slowed down, stopping in a small clearing where he dropped to his knees. As Meat got closer, he realized Window was crying.

"What's wrong?" Meat rested his hand on Window's heaving back.

Window shook his head as he cleared his nose.

"Did you get any on you?" Meat tried to lighten the situation.

Window laughed. "Why won't you leave me alone?"

"Who else would I bug then? Einstein? Billie-Bob?"

"I saw how you looked at her."

"Who?"

"You know who, that girl, what's her name, Maria?"

"So, when was the last time you saw a girl like that? And Anna doesn't count." It was a known fact Window had a crush on Anna. Of course, all the boys did, Meat included. Anna had her sights set on Ritchie, who worked with one of the scavenger crews and barely recognized her. It was rumored that he was gay and lived with an older man on the outskirts of the growing town. A couple of more things that hadn't changed. Human nature's desire to have what one could not possess, and the need for gossip.

"Anna, the dreams I've had about that one." Window pushed himself to his feet.

"What happened back there? Why did you freeze up? I've never seen that happen to you before."

"She reminded me of my mom."

"You remember your mom?"

Window nodded and sadness once more clouded his eyes. "Of course, I remember my mom. I should, I killed her."

Meat stepped back stunned. It wasn't every day a friend admitted to matricide. Even in their current situation, an act like that was not normal.

"My dad was pretty smart. He was what they called a Prepper. When the shit hit the fan, he took my mom, who was pregnant with me, into the hills outside Richmond where he had a small cabin on a little lake. It was there that I was born. I don't remember much about my early life.

"I recall my dad teaching me how to shoot when I was young. He gave me a little twenty-two pistol. I could barely hold it up. I practiced with that thing every day while my dad hunted or fished, cured hides, or tended to our little garden in the back. We felt safe there, or so we thought.

"The week before my sixth birthday, a stranger came to us. He had been shot and was losing blood fast. My mom and dad tried to save him, it was no use, he died. The next day a group of men on horseback arrived looking for the man who they claimed had stolen from them. My dad took them out back to show them the grave, they had an argument, somebody shouted, and the shooting started. They killed my dad. We were hiding inside, my Mom and me, when they came looking for us." Window stopped and took a deep, shuddering breath as the memory washed through him.

Meat placed his hand on Window's shoulder. "You don't have to keep going if you don't want to.".

Window shook his head. "I have to. I gotta get this out of me. I've been keeping it bottled up for the past seven years and it's eating me alive. Last night when I saw that woman, it was like I was back at the cabin.

"They raped my mom, took her into the back room where I couldn't see what was happening, I knew from the sounds they were hurting her, and I wanted to help. I had my twenty-two and pulled it out. They thought it was funny and laughed when I aimed it at them. One of them snatched the twenty-two from my hand and handed me my father's pistol."

Window pulled the forty-four from its holster and ran his finger along the design carved into the barrel. "It was still loaded."

"The last one came out of the back room pulling up his pants. He told the others he'd strangled her, and they all laughed. After a bit, she came out, nearly nude, her dress torn, the cord the man had used to strangle her still wrapped around her neck. They told me I had to shoot her quick, to give her peace. I'd fired the forty-four several times before with my dad, so I knew what to expect. There were five rounds in the chamber. I saved the last one for her.

"Everything happened so fast they hardly had time to react. The last man I shot knocked over the kerosene lantern and a fire started in the cabin. My mom staggered towards me, that cord still tight around her neck and I remember wondering how she could still be breathing with it like that. Then I realized she wasn't really alive anymore, so I shot her, and ran away.

"I didn't have time to do anything. I couldn't change out of my pajamas. My mom had wanted me to know what it was like to be a kid, so she made me a pair of Batman pajamas. My dad found a comic bookstore, I was familiar with Batman and Superman, along with the Fantastic Four, Hulk, Spiderman, and a bunch of other superheroes. It was how I learned to read.

"They wanted me to know what it was like to be a kid, to have the same kind of childhood they had." Tears rolled down Window's cheeks and Meat remained quiet, though a bit uncomfortable. It wasn't easy listening to another's confessions.

"Then you found your way to the Bluff?" Meat said.

Window shook his head. "When I came out of the cabin, my dad was staggering towards the front door. I didn't have any rounds left so I turned and ran into the forest. I don't know how long I ran. In the morning, I realized I was completely lost with no idea which way to go. I set up a camp, those things my father taught me found their way through the fear, and as night came, I saw a faint glow to the west. I followed it for three days, drinking stump water and getting sick, trying unsuccessfully to catch something to eat, failing miserably in nearly everything I tried to do.

"On the fourth morning, I found Bremo Bluff. If I missed it I would have died."

Window became silent, his emotions spent on the telling of the tale. It was a silence Meat didn't want to interrupt. One day, he would confess his own sins, for now, that day lay somewhere in an uncertain future.

16

By the time Meat and Window returned to the house, the dark clouds had thinned enough to allow the sunshine through and the day that started cold and dreary promised to end on a high note. The forest around them was alive with the chatter of life as birds and squirrels moved among branches sprouting new leaves.

Spring was gearing up with the promise of renewal as Mother Nature ramped it up a few notches. It was another of the many truths of the world. No matter what happened, nature would continue following its predetermined course. The death that was winter would continue to bring the snow and cold winds that would always be followed by the rebirth of spring.

Gregory and the others were gathered around the picnic table, soaking up the warming rays of the sun, and as they crossed the backyard, Einstein jumped from his seat and ran to them.

"Is he okay?" Einstein nodded in Window's direction.

"He'll be all right," Meat said. "What about you?"

Einstein shrugged, stuffing his hands into his pockets. "After you left, Gregory talked to me, pointing something out that should have been obvious to me."

"Oh?"

"If Window really wanted to kill me, he would have done so already."

"He's got a pretty good point."

"He said something else too."

"What's that?"

"He said he didn't feel it would be a good idea for Maria to come with us."

"I'll have to agree with him on that," Meat said.

Window joined them and stuck his hand out to Einstein. "I'm sorry about what happened last night."

Einstein pushed aside his hand and wrapped him in a hug. "It's all right, man, I understand." Stepping back, Einstein turned to Meat. "What are we going to do with her?"

"Do with who?" Window said.

"Gregory doesn't believe it's a good idea for Maria to come with us," Einstein said.

"I suggest we leave her here with Billie-Bob. We've got Gregory, and he wants revenge," Meat said.

"We're not looking for revenge. We only want to get the children back, that's all."

Meat shook his head. "I wish it was that simple. They know where Bremo Bluff is. They know what's in the compound. Remember what they told us in class."

Einstein held up his hand. "I know. We can never let anyone know about Bremo Bluff. No one can ever leave," he recited in a robotic monotone. "But they have. What about the Jenkins family, they left last fall?"

Meat shook his head. "I talked to one of the guys who escorted them out. Sure, they left the compound, only they didn't get very far."

"You're lying," Einstein shouted, stepping back as shock skewed his features.

Einstein's outburst drew the attention of those still seated at the picnic table. Gregory started to get up and Meat motioned for him to stay. This was his problem and he would handle it.

"I spoke with the council before we left. They gave us their blessing for this little trip and guaranteed us a scavenging spot if we rescue the children, they stipulated we can't leave any survivors. It's a matter of survival. About what's best for the greater good."

"We take in survivors," Einstein said.

"Of course, we do, and many choose to stay. Those that don't are allowed to leave but they don't get very far."

"How do you know all this, and I don't?"

"Because they told me. That's the way it's been since the beginning. Yes, we will take in survivors, but once someone knows about the compound, they can't be trusted to keep their mouths shut."

"What about us? We know about the compound. We've been allowed to leave."

"They know we'll be back, it's the only real home we've ever known. Haven't you noticed it's only the people who have been in the compound the longest that can scavenge?"

"No, it can't be, I know they've let newcomers out to scavenge," Einstein said, clutching at straws, the realization that Meat was right slowly dawning in his eyes. If only he'd be honest with himself, then he would see the truth.

"Name one," Meat said as he crossed his arms over his chest.

Outwardly, Bremo Bluff looked like a paradise on earth, especially to anyone who had struggled to survive beyond its fences. It offered safety and security, the warmth of human contact, a roof over the head and a warm meal in the belly.

Like many of the silver linings we discover in life, at its heart lay a secret.

For everything we take, something must be given in return, for what we give we receive as it is in all facets of life. Karma rested upon the razor's edge of a finely crafted blade, balanced by the give and take that made the world go around. The compound had survived as long as it had for two reasons. It was off the beaten path, and it kept the knowledge of its existence close. Like a poker player will keep a good hand close so no one can see what they have. It was how they managed to survive as long as they had.

Meat understood this with a wisdom that exceeded his years. Einstein, for all his smarts, still had a naïve view of the world around them. Born at Bremo Bluff, he'd never experienced the uncertainty Meat had grown up with. Never sure when, where, or even what, you would eat next.

While the man he called dad had done a tremendous job keeping him safe, he could still recall days of wanting. The desire for a hot meal, a warm place to sleep, the ability to let one's guard down completely and totally relax. It was no way for a child to grow up. But what choice did any of them really have?

"I give up," Einstein said as he threw up his hands and walked away.

"Is he gonna be all right?" Window said.

"I hope so," Meat said as he turned back to the others still gathered around the picnic table.

As they approached, Gregory got to his feet and met them before they could reach the picnic table. "I didn't want anyone else to hear this, I don't believe it's a good idea for Maria to come with us."

"You'll get no argument from me. I decided the same thing," Meat said. "I was going to leave Billie-Bob here to protect her until we returned, then she can come to our compound with us."

"What about me? Am I invited?"

"Everyone is welcome, you do realize that once you know the details of our camp, you can never leave."

"Three hots, and a cot, right?" Gregory said with a wink.

"What does that mean?" Window said.

"It's an old saying from before. It's used to describe prison. Three hot meals and a cot to sleep on. I'll have to sleep on your offer. Don't know if I'm willing to give up my freedom yet."

Meat shrugged, realizing that Gregory had come pretty damned close to describing what they had at the Bluff. For the first time, he considered what the lights at night really meant. Watchtowers stood every fifty yards or so along the fence, manned by men with high-powered rifles and spotlights. Many times, as he lay in bed at night, listening for the occasional rifle shot that would be explained away the following morning as the killing of a wandering zombie. No one ever questioned that explanation, no one ever asked to see the body, and occasionally, one of the inhabitants would report that one of their family members was missing.

It all became chillingly clear and his loyalty to the people who ran Bremo Bluff was called into question. He couldn't let anyone else see the doubt he felt. For now, his personal feelings would remain his own little secret.

"Billie-Bob, I need you to stay with Maria until we come back through, then we'll return to the Bluff."

"I wanted to see Richmond," Billie-Bob said.

"I'll stay with her," Einstein said.

Is that a good idea? Meat wondered. Einstein had been shocked to discover the truth about Bremo Bluff, a truth that Meat suspected long before he'd learned about it himself. It was quid pro quo. If you wanted to be safe, protected from all the bad things that existed beyond the fence, you had to give up something in return.

Was the chance to live a free life beyond the fence an equal trade? It was a question there was no ready answer for. Anything one wanted in life had to be traded for. If you wanted to eat, you learned to hunt, and took the time to do so. If you wanted protection from the weather, you built a house.

Billie-Bob was the best they had for long-range shots, which worked wonders in the open, would his special talent come in handy in a city? Meat had never seen Richmond. Not even a picture. Those who survived were not concerned with photo albums when they fled the zombie hordes. He had an old roadmap to guide them. On one side was a picture, faded with age and use, a row of tall buildings gleaming in the sunlight, reflected from the surface of a river.

Of secondary concern, would Einstein take this opportunity to flee? He doubted it. Bremo Bluff was the only safe haven any of them really knew. He'd have to take that chance, burn that bridge when he came to it, as old man Sawyers was fond of saying.

"Okay, Billie-Bob, you're coming to Richmond. Einstein, stay with Maria, keep a low profile, don't draw attention to yourselves. We should be back within a week. If we don't make it, return to the Bluffs, and let them know what happened."

17

Penny leaned on the glass counter at Ted's hardware store. She was exhausted, it had been nearly a week since she'd had a good night's sleep, and every time she closed her eyes the images from that old nightmare returned. In it she was alone in town, the sound of horse's hooves coming from all around her, the bodies of the townspeople hanging from the streetlights lining every street. People she knew, people she had grown up with, stared at her from the other side of death. Eyes wide and glassy, tongues protruding from slack lips, watching her as she fled from the riders on horseback hunting her. She was the last one alive. The only witness to an atrocity committed by demons from hell sent to find her because she refused to believe.

"God has called the faithful home, and the sinners who remain must face their torment." Reverend Wood's words whispered through her mind. From a sermon she attended when she was much younger. The reverend was no longer alive, having followed his wife and young daughter into the death that plagued the land.

"Earth to Penny," Ted said, and Penny turned to face the young man behind the counter. He was two years her senior and she felt lucky he'd chosen her from the few females his age that were available. He winked as he helped the customer before him.

"Now you make sure you give me exactly a pound, I don't wanna pay a penny more than I have to." Mrs. Hardett watched the scale carefully as Ted poured the corn meal into the small paper bag.

"Yes Ma'am," Ted replied, glancing at Penny with a scowl before his gaze dropped to her breast.

"Don't give it away, sweetie, make em pay for it," Mrs. Hardett said, "kids these days don't understand. In my day we…"

"Will there be anything else, Mrs. Hardett?" Ted interrupted her before she could launch into another one of her rants.

"That'll be all for today, Teddy, "put that on my tab, please."

"I'm sorry Mrs. Hardett, Dad said not to put anything else on your tab till you made a payment."

"But I was in yesterday and made a payment, dropped off four bushels of corn, they're over on the table to be sold."

"He never said anything to me Mrs. Hardett."

"I'm sorry, Ted, that's my fault." Ted's dad stepped out of the back room carrying a box he placed on the counter in front of Penny. "Hi Penny." He smiled before turning to Mrs. Hardett. "Forgive me Mrs. Hardett, I forgot to mark down what you bought in, put her cornmeal on her tab Ted."

"Yes sir," Ted said as he slid the bag across the counter to Mrs. Hardett, "I'm sorry Mrs. Hardett."

"That's okay, Teddy, these things happen. You really need to make an honest woman out of that one," she said as she took the cornmeal and nodded at Penny leaning on the counter. She turned and walked out of the store.

"Ted, I need you to sort these bullets, put em in packs of five, and price them the same as the others."

"Do you need me to break down the ten packs."

"You better. I think this is the last for this area, had to scrounge for these so we'll have to make them last."

"I'll help," Penny said and reached into the box to pull out a handful of assorted bullets.

"What the hell," Ted's dad said, and Penny looked up to see a group of riders enter the town.

"You kids stay here," he said as he retrieved his pistol from under the counter and stepped out onto the front stoop. A small crowd had gathered around the arrivals and when Penny crossed to the window, she spotted Jamie astride one of Mel Conner's horses.

"What's he doing here?"

"Who?"

"Jamie."

"Jamie's here?" Ted stepped around the counter and joined her at the large picture window facing main street. The crowd around the riders had grown until it seemed everyone who lived in town had turned out. Jamie was scanning the crowd, and when his gaze settled on her she took several steps back as terror blossomed in the pit of her stomach. "We better get out of here."

"Who's with Jamie?" Ted said as he waved at the crowd beyond the window. Realizing Penny was no longer at his side he turned to her.

"What's wrong?"

A splash of blood stained the side of the horse Jamie rode and when he pointed at her, she nearly fainted when one of the men with him turned to look in her direction. His features though normal, reminded her of the demons that were haunting her sleep.

"We have to get out of here, now." Penny pulled Ted towards the back room.

"Why? What's wrong with you?"

"Why are you on Mel's horse?" Ted's dad said from the front stoop. It was the last thing he said before the world erupted in gunfire and screams. His body flung back through the front door he stepped through only moments before.

"Dad?" Ted stared down at his dead father as Penny screamed.

"Dad!" Ted crossed to his father, his gaze never leaving his face as Penny pulled at him for follow her.

"Dad." He tried to kneel next to his father's lifeless body, but Penny pulled him away. More gunfire came from outside, followed by shouts and screams, and running feet as the people fled.

Penny dragged Ted through the back room and into the alley behind the building. He stumbled as they crossed the muddy lane and the sound of horse's hooves on pavement came from the end of the street. She looked up to see Jamie on the other side of the muddy lane. He dug his heels in the horse's flanks and it leapt at her with a shriek of pain and terror.

"Leave her alone," Ted shouted, stepping between Penny and Jamie with his hands raised to stop Jamie. The horse reared back, hooves flailed, and Ted was driven to the ground beneath the combined weight of Jamie and the horse. Penny ran, the image of Ted being crushed beneath the horses' hooves trapped in her mind as pounding hooves pursued her like the demons from her dream.

At the end of the lane she darted left, into the Morrison's garage, and clawed her way through years of accumulated debris. She reached the door that led to their backyard, and the safety of a place she was intimately familiar with when Jamie's voice came from behind.

"Why you running from me? You know you want me. You've always wanted me. I know you were using Ted to make me jealous, and that's all right, I won't hold it against you."

"Get away from me. Why did you hurt him? Why did you kill Ted?"

"But you don't care about Ted. I know you don't

"Stay away from me." She yanked at the door to the Morrison's back yard as the sound of Jamie pushing his way through the debris came from behind her. She spun around, grabbing the first thing that came to hand, an old golf club with a large wooden head.

"Stay back or I'll kill you."

Jamie stopped, "you're confused, it'll all make sense in time, now give me the golf club."

She realized the shooting and shouting had stopped. The sounds of the distant fight replaced by the steady approach of several horses. They're coming for her, the demons from her dream were coming to get her.

"Leave me alone," she screamed, swinging the golf club at Jamie's head, the wooden end bounced off the wall of the garage, the shaft vibrating in her hands.

"Can't you control your woman, boy." A cold voice came from behind Jamie.

"I've got everything under control," Jamie said, twisting around to speak with the unseen arrival.

"Don't look that way to me." The comment was punctuated by the click of a hammer being drawn back on a pistol.

"I told you I'd handle it," Jamie said.

Penny threw herself at Jamie, kicking and screaming, swinging the golf club wildly. Driving him back out of the garage. She followed, the image of Ted lying dead in the street fueling her rage. Like a trapped animal she turned on her tormentor, and Jamie backed away from her attack, one hand over his head the other trying to protect his body as she drove him from the garage. \

She followed, swinging the golf club wildly, until it was yanked out of her hand and she found herself surrounded by four men on horseback. They watched her from beneath wide brimmed hats, eyes as cold as ice, and she looked from one to the other, slowly becoming aware that they were not of this world.

There was something off about their features, they each had two eyes, a nose, and a mouth, along with an ear on either side of their head, but the proportions seemed off. The spacing between each feature slightly different than it was on the faces she was accustomed to seeing. Their faces were wider, squatter, their head forming an oval lying on its side. The jaw long, jutting out from the bottom of the face like a small shelf.

"Control your woman," the man on her left said as his horse shifted position. Even the horses seemed off, unlike the horses she knew. They were shorter, squat, wide.

"I'm not his woman."

The muzzle of a pistol settled against her ear. "There's no need for you to live."

"No, don't, I promised I would help." Jamie pushed the pistol aside, crowding in close to whisper in her ear. "If you want to live, do as I say."

"She'll come around, I promise," Jamie said while shielding her body with his own.

With her mind's eye she saw Ted lying on the ground, broken, trampled beneath the hooves of Jamie's horse. She saw his dad lying on the floor of the hardware store. She heard the screams of the people she had grown up with, and she looked up at the mounted riders around her. She wanted to die, she wanted to join the others, her friends and family.

Only she couldn't. She understood this now, it all made a strange sort of sense, the nightmares that had been plaguing her. They were preparing her for this day. Getting her ready for the biggest challenge of her life. If she was to exact vengeance for what they'd done, she had to keep breathing, she had to keep living, if only to remember those she loved.

With great difficulty she nodded, the two factions within warring against one another. She would go with them, and when they least expected it, she would have her revenge.

"I knew you'd come around, come on, let's go. I've gotta do this thing for them, then we can settle down someplace safe."

"What do you have to do?" She tried to sound natural, relaxed, but her words came out stiff and emotionless. When Jamie placed his hand on her shoulder, she mentally recoiled from his touch while keeping a smile on her face. She imagined what it was going to be like to cut his hand off and her smile widened.

"I knew you'd come around," Jamie said as he led her to his horse. "We'll get a horse for you, and you won't have to double up with me. I'm gonna show these guys around, they're looking for someone, but they're not from this area."

"Where are they from?"

Jamie leaned in close and whispered in her ear, his rancid breath gagging her. "I think they're from heaven."

If they were from heaven, they should already know their way around. She had no idea where Jamie got that notion. She was confident they were demons from hell and had lied to Jamie. Everyone knew he wasn't the brightest bulb in the box. She allowed herself to be led to the waiting horse where Jamie climbed into the saddle and leaned over to give her a hand. She would wait. A time would come when they let their guard down, and she'd be ready.

She glanced to the rider on her left and noticed he was watching her intently. He nodded with understanding and smiled, if what he did with his lips could be called that. Baring his teeth in a wide grimace that did little to comfort her.

18

Towering trees lined the road on either of Billie-Bob, the branches interlaced above his head, created a living tunnel as route six passed into what had once been known as Tuckahoe. On both sides of the road, empty houses sat behind overgrown lawns, silent sentinels watching over the comings and goings of the ghosts of the past. Their windows like empty eyes, hiding in shadowed depths the memories of the terror the occupants must have felt when they realized the end was upon them.

One house stood out for Billie-Bob, and he expected his uncle to step out from behind the front door with a smile and a wave. His true nature hidden behind a friendly façade. Memories stirred and he furrowed his brow as he focused on the words of an old story his mother used to read to him every night.

"They roared their terrible roars and gnashed their terrible teeth and rolled their terrible eyes and showed their terrible claws." The words comforted him and helped to keep the memories at bay. With his mind's eye, he saw the small room he once shared with his mother. The warm glow of a candle on the table offered enough illumination to keep the darkness at bay. An open window allowed a gentle breeze to stir lace curtains yellowed with age, carrying with it the scent of freshly turned earth and the biting chill of winter's recent passing. He sat on her lap, his brother snuggled next to him, wrapped in a blanket and her arms, the book open on their lap as she read the familiar story.

"They roared their terrible roars and gnashed their terrible teeth and rolled their terrible eyes and showed their terrible claws," he whispered as her voice recited the passage in his mind. He repeated the passage, the memory of her arms around him providing a measure of comfort as he followed Meat and Window through the living tunnel.

"I know the passage." Gregory came up beside him.

"It's from a book my mom used to read to me any time I got scared," Billie-Bob said as the memory faded. Safety lay in the memory of his mother's loving arms, and he regretted losing her.

"I read the same book to my daughter when she was little."

"Really?"

"Yeah, really, are you all right?"

"Yeah, I'm fine, why do you ask?"

Gregory shook his head. "No reason. No, let me be honest, I'm worried about your well-being. You keep repeating the passage to yourself over and over again. Like a Tibetan monk chanting a prayer."

"I didn't realize I was doing it. It's the only part of the book I remember, and it makes me feel better."

"Fair enough, are you sure there's nothing else?"

Billie-Bob's gaze was drawn to a house that looked like his uncle's. The door was about to swing open, and his uncle would step out, and it would start all over again. He shook his head, pushing away the memories clamoring for his attention as he tried to lose himself in his mother's words, repeating the passage in his mind.

"You're doing it again."

"What?"

"Mouthing the words."

"Was I?"

"Yeah, it's kind of spooky, if you ask me."

"Did you ever wonder if maybe none of this really happened?" Billie-Bob said.

"What do you mean?"

"What if it's an experiment?"

"Where did you get that idea?"

"A guy I know at the Bluffs, he works in the metal shop. He's kind of weird and most everyone else leaves him alone. I think he's pretty cool, though. He has some crazy ideas about the government."

"Like conspiracy theories?"

"Yeah, he believes the awakening was caused by something he called Chemtrails."

Gregory smiled as he nodded. "I've heard it before."

"It could be true?"

"I guess anything's possible."

"He also believes the awakening was not as widespread as it was reported, it only happened in isolated areas the government was keeping secured. Like we're some big experiment and if we walked long enough in one direction, we'd come to a wall watched over by armed guards."

"Sounds like a movie that came out when I was young, if it's true, what would they tell the rest of the world to keep them out?"

Billie-Bob shrugged. "Mark says they could use any excuse from a chemical leak to radiation to keep people out."

"There are too many holes in the theory. I mean, what about satellites? The United States wasn't the only country with satellites in space."

"What's a satellite?"

"No one told you about satellites?"

"We only learned what we needed to know to survive. If it couldn't feed us, clothe us, or provide shelter, why learn about it?"

"Aren't you curious about how the world worked before?"

"Sure, but what good would a satellite do me now?"

Gregory shrugged. "Not much, I guess."

"I'd rather learn about grocery stores, something I can use. Man, wouldn't it be great to find a grocery store that hasn't been looted yet?"

"Now you are reaching, and even if you did, most of the food wouldn't be any good."

"It would be full of canned goods and they'd still be edible."

"You've got a point there."

"Hey, did I tell you about the zombie who visited a whorehouse?"

"Yeah. He wanted his money back because he couldn't get it up. He had DD, dead dick."

"Hey, that's my line."

"You need some new material, kid." Gregory pushed ahead to catch up with Meat and Window.

Billie-Bob watched him go. "They roared their terrible roars and gnashed their terrible teeth and rolled their terrible eyes and showed their terrible claws," he whispered.

His thoughts turned to Mark, and the stories he'd told him of the world before the awakening. The war on terrorists, the government and how it was using its power to keep people prisoner. He'd escaped from Richmond during the initial outbreak and would tell anyone who listened about how ruthless the military had been. In Billie-Bob, he'd found a rapt audience and had filled his head with all manner of odd tales about power and the greed it bred.

All Roads Lead to Terror

The same kind of power those who ran the compound at the Bluff held. He hadn't been surprised when Meat told them the truth about Bremo Bluff. In fact, the stories Mark had shared led him to suspect that those in charge of the bluff really did not have their best interests at heart.

It was becoming too much to dwell on, so he returned to his comfort zone. "They roared their terrible roars and gnashed their terrible teeth and rolled their terrible eyes and showed their terrible claws," he whispered as his mother's soothing voice filled his mind.

19

As evening descended, they set up camp on the roof of an apartment building providing a view of downtown Richmond. Two days had passed since they left Einstein and Maria. Two days in which they had not crossed paths with any other survivors as they traveled through a dead world. The signs of their passage all around him, as was the fading sign of their quarry. On the first night, they built a fire on the blackened spot where the group they followed had built one the night before. Meat knew it was them based on the footprints around the fire, the thread of small boots mingled with larger soft-soled shoes.

The city laid spread out before them, low buildings close, rising to towering buildings of glass scraping the sky. The purple haze of night marched across the sky from the east, stars twinkling against a black backdrop, in sharp contrast to the fading hues of red and orange burning along the horizon to the west.

In the center of Richmond, several of the high-rise buildings burned with the flickering glow of nearby fires as the fading light cast long shadows. Other high rises remained dark and foreboding, dead monoliths shrouded in the shadows of the past. The James River was like a bejeweled serpent slithering through the heart of downtown Richmond, its surface reflecting the dancing lights of the fires burning within that desolate place.

Screams came from the streets buried in the deeper shadows, cries of anger and anguish mingling in a nightly ritual speaking to them on a dark and primitive level. An oppressive air hung over the city, calling to their dark primal psyche as it beckoned for them to come on, even as it warned them away.

"I'll take first watch," Meat said as they gazed at the city from their vantage point. The night was clear, and warm enough for them to sleep beneath the stars. "Billie-Bob, wake Window, who will wake up Gregory when it's time." Gregory nodded as he swung his pack off his shoulders, resting his rifle on the pack as he wandered to the edge of the roof with a pair of binoculars.

From the parking lot six stories below came the sound of running feet punctuated by shouts.

"Leave me be!" An old man's voice floated up to them as the running footsteps stopped.

"Give it to me, old man," someone said.

Meat knelt and looked over the top of the short wall running the circumference of the roof. Three teens had cornered an older man against the rusted fence surrounding the parking area. He was clutching something in his hands, holding it close, protecting it with his body.

Billie-Bob lifted his rifle and sighted down the scope, settling the butt in his shoulder.

"Don't." Meat held out his hand.

"I can take all three of them."

"And bring how many more?" Meat whispered. Sometimes, it didn't pay to be a hero. As much as he hated to admit it, the old man was on his own. They could help, only there was no way to know how many others the sound of their shots would bring. They had to remain focused on the task at hand, to save the children—getting sidetracked by a running fight wouldn't help.

They watched and waited as the scene played out below them.

"You can't have it," the old man yelled as he struggled to maintain his grip on the object.

The old man kicked out, catching one of the teens squarely between the legs, doubling him over as the other two laughed at their friend's misfortune. The teen slowly collapsed to the ground as they turned their attention from their victim.

"He got ya good, Tyrone."

Carefully, the old man sidestepped away from the teens, when he was a full ten feet away, he turned and ran down the street, vanishing into the shadows.

One of the teens looked up. "He's getting away. Get back here, you old fuck."

Footsteps pounded across the pavement below them as the two teens chased the old man down the street. They vanished into the thick shadows, pounding footsteps fading into the distance, their shouts becoming remote whispers in the night. The last teen slowly pushed himself to his feet and staggered after his friends.

Night fell completely as Meat settled in for the first watch as the others dropped off to sleep. It was amazing what a little walking could do to wear a person out. Meat struggled against the call of sleep as he gazed out from his perch at the edge of the roof. Every so often he would look back at the door they had used as access. They had blocked it to keep anyone from following them, one could never be too careful when you ventured into the wilds of this new world.

20

Meat woke up with a start, looking around from his vantage point, half expecting to find himself surrounded by those who would do him harm. He'd drifted off to sleep and was a bit disoriented by his sudden waking. He'd been dreaming of a shadowy hallway again and a chill whispered down his spine as he recalled the doorway at the end. A narrow strip of light had shown under the door, while from behind the peeling face came the familiar sound of rats cavorting across a hardwood floor, tiny claws clicking against old wood. He shivered again at the image, wrapping his arms about himself as the night flowed silently around him.

The waning moon cast the city into a contrasting patchwork of light and shadows. Nothing had changed—fires still burned in the distance and an occasional cry echoed across the dark face of the city. The others slept, huddled close to one another, wrapped in sleeping bags showing the wear of continued use.

Glancing at the watch on his wrist, a cheap wind up affair that lasted longer than he imagined possible, he realized he'd only been on guard for an hour. He'd probably been asleep nearly the entire time. Taking a deep breath, he focused his attention on the vacant street below as his mind wandered and his eyelids once more grew heavy.

Faced with the task before them, the reality of what they planned to do staring him in the face, doubts he had struggled so hard to keep suppressed rose to the surface.

What if I'm wrong? He worried as he gazed sleepily at the street below. What if I get everybody killed? In Bremo Bluff when he'd first considered going out after the kidnapped children, the possibility of something bad happening to them wasn't very high among his concerns.

He'd looked upon the expedition with an excitement only a child could muster, a blind anticipation that ignored the doubts whispering in the back of his mind. Standing upon the threshold of achieving their objective of finding the missing children and returning them to Bremo Bluff, the doubts gnawed at him.

He'd never before felt as alone as he did at this moment.

Strip away the false bravado and all you had left was a scared little kid. Yeah, he knew how to survive, he knew how to defend himself, and had done so on a number of occasions. The fact remained, he, Window, and Billie-Bob, were only kids. He hadn't even started shaving yet and here he was leading a group on a quest that could get them all killed.

He was so damned tired. His eyelids slid down as his head slowly dropped to his chest, so sleepy.

A sound on the street below brought him fully awake and he peered into the thick shadows crouched along the buildings bordering the street. He strained to see what was hidden, his mind filling in the blanks for what he couldn't see. Anyone who has had the misfortune of guarding a desolate place at night understands when they're alone in the dark, how the mind tends to play tricks on them. They see things that aren't there.

From the street below came the steady sound of footsteps, a hard heel ringing against the pavement with a *clip-clop* sound echoing from the shadowed faces of the buildings lining the street. Someone was walking down the street, alone, at a leisurely pace that begged for someone with less than honest intentions to come along. A lone figure moved in the black depths of the shadows as the footsteps became louder.

A solitary figure stepped into the moonlight painting the intersection with an effervescent white light, his shadow cast along the ground at his feet, vanishing into the thick shadows crowded against the base of the buildings, connecting him to the shadowy depths that birthed him.

He stood in the intersection, tall and slender, staring up at Meat, who could feel the stranger's eyes on him, probing him, searching the dark nooks and crannies of his mind where all manner of self-doubt and fear resided.

He's only a kid. The words blossomed in his mind. With them came a primitive fear of the unknown, of shadowy places shrouded in perpetual twilight. The image of a vast, desolate landscape filled his mind. Thick clouds swollen with the promise of rain passed over the face of this bleak expanse of nothing. A lonely figure moved across the blasted place, a shadowy wraith flitting to and fro as it approached, dancing across the landscape with a wild abandon.

A hand fell on his shoulder and Meat jerked awake, one hand pulling the knife he carried from its scabbard at his waist as his head swiveled around in search of who had touched him.

"It's all right, man, it's only me," Window took several steps back as Meat jumped to his feet and swung around with the knife in his hand.

"Where did he go?" Meat said.

"Where did who go?"

"The man." Meat was still gathering his thoughts as he struggled to put together a coherent picture of the world around him. He spun back around and stepped over to the edge of the roof, his gaze fixed on the moonlit intersection below. Nothing moved in the moonlight, no sound save the stirring of a gentle breeze as it whispered across the edge of the roof and caressed his face with chilled fingers that carried a hint of winter's recent passing.

"A man was down there." Meat pointed at the intersection.

Window shook his head as he glanced down at the street. "You were asleep."

"I was?"

"You must have been dreaming."

"It felt so real."

"What did he want?"

"Who?"

"The man from your dream, what did he want?"

"I don't know." Meat shrugged as he sat back down.

Window sat down beside him. "You can go to sleep. I'll take over for you."

"I'll be all right. Why are you awake?"

Window shrugged. "I don't know, I had this sudden feeling someone was in trouble and I needed to help them."

"Who was in trouble?"

"I don't know. I had this feeling something was wrong."

"I'm glad you did."

"Why? What happened?"

Meat watched the distant fires burn around the high rises at the center of the city, his doubts stirring, filling him with questions that had no easy answers. He sensed the end of their quest was near.

Tomorrow, or possibly the following day, it would be over. They would have the children back and return to Bremo Bluff heroes, or all of them would die.

"I think I might have bitten off more than I can chew."

"Are you worried about tomorrow?"

Meat nodded. "Aren't you?"

"They've already taken everything I cared for. The only thing left is my life, and they can have that as well."

"That's a pretty dismal view. I mean, we're only kids, really, we're nothing more than children ourselves. We've got our whole lives ahead of us."

"I quit being a kid the moment my mother died. And what we have is only what they left us. Which isn't much, a dead world filled with bad things."

"We control the future. We are the future."

"And that's why you'll survive, you have hope."

"What about the others?" Meat nodded towards Gregory and Billie-Bob.

"I don't think we'll have to worry about Gregory. Billie-Bob might freeze up on us, Gregory will be an asset. He has the same look."

"What look is that?"

"The I-don't-give-a-fuck look. They've taken everything from him, and he has less to live for than I do."

Window had a point. In a fight, it was usually the one who had the least to live for that stood the best chance of winning. After all, they were willing to take the greatest risk. He only hoped when tomorrow came, all of them were ready for whatever was thrown at them.

21

Sleep eluded Penny as she lay in bed, the events of the day replaying themselves in her mind. Jamie was asleep in the bed next to hers, snoring lightly as the night slowly passed around her. He'd tried to get her to join him, but she begged off, claiming she was still upset over what happened. Not to mention they were not yet married. If the men they accompanied were angles, would they not frown on them sleeping together. Was it not a sin to have sex outside of marriage?

Jamie agreed, reluctantly, and she tucked him in with a few lingering touches to keep him interested. Not that she needed to bother. He was taken with her, and a small part of her cringed at what she planned to do when the opportunity presented itself. Every time she felt her resolve waver, she remembered Ted lying in the mud.

They never bothered to bury their victims, leaving them lie where they fell. Outside nocturnal creatures emerged from the night to feed on the bounty provided and it stoked the fires of her need for revenge. Dogs growled over the leavings and she clamped her hands over her ears to block out the sound.

Where were the others? She wondered and carefully climbed out of bed so as not to disturb Jamie. At the door she paused for a moment and watched as Jamie slept, his chest rising and falling with a steady rhythm. Assured he was still asleep she stepped into the hallway.

All Roads Lead to Terror

They had taken over Reverend Wood's residence and she moved confidently down the dark hallway. As a child she and Rebecca, the reverend's daughter, played hide and seek, searching for each other through the many rooms of the reverend's house. Thoughts of Becca elicited a deep sadness. The world was moving on and Becca had not survived long in this new world. She caught a cold the year she turned nine, and it evolved into full blown pneumonia. Had it happened before the awakening a trip to the doctor would have saved her. As it was, before anyone could do anything to help her, she drowned in her own fluids. After the funeral Becca's mother returned to Becca's room where she took her own life. As the memories washed through her Penny moved down the hallway. The walls around her had once known so much happiness, now they were shrouded in the darkness of despair, the ghosts of the past whispering from shadowed places.

At the door to Becca's old room she stopped, certain she'd heard the soft squeak of the bed from behind a door the Reverend never opened again. She only knew this because after the funeral for Becca's mother the town had shown up to comfort him in his hour of need. While the adults gathered in the dining room and kitchen, and the kids played outside, Penny snuck upstairs.

She didn't know why she did it, maybe she was hoping to see Becca one last time. She went into Becca's room, and as she sat on the side of the bed, like she had when Becca fell ill, a cold chill gathered around her. A shadow fell across her, blocking the sunlight coming through the window, and when she looked up, she'd seen the ghost of Becca's mother hanging from the frayed end of a rope that had not been taken down.

She screamed, again, and again. Pounding feet and voices came from below as she cried out and Becca's mom stared at her with bulging eyes, the shriveled tip of her tongue protruding from the corner of her lips.

Penny shuddered as the memory washed over her and turned away from the door, not wanting to experience that again.

At the end of the hall stairs led to the first floor and a faint light glowed from below. She heard voices, the scrape of a chair, heavy footsteps that moved towards the front of the house. She peered around the corner and spotted one of her captors as he looked outside, his hand resting on the butt of the revolver sticking out of the holster on his hip.

She traced the designs on his leather vest, the swirling lines and converging circles that made her feel lightheaded. A soft pecking, keeping time with the beat of her heart, came from behind her left eye and she rubbed it to no avail. The pain grew from a faint pecking to a steady pounding that forced her to look away.

Who are these people? She rubbed her temples to massage away the pain, but it persisted. Growing more intense until it felt like a spike was being driven into the center of her forehead. Clinging to the corner, a soft moan in her throat, she realized the man at the door had turned and was watching her. She saw his eyes beneath the brim of his wide hat, glowing with a soft red light.

She staggered back, wanting to flee, while at the same time curious. He climbed the steps to where she stood, and she found her feet had taken root in the threadbare carpet. He reached for her, caressing her face with one coarse hand as an inhuman desire overwhelmed her. Images flashed through her mind, old scenes from the past that spoke to her in an ancient voice. They were *Teka,* these men who rode alone, sworn to protect a queen, and enforce her laws. Bred for that reason and no other. Trained from the day they could walk they were taught one thing, and one thing only.

To kill.

Her hand fell to the pistol on his hip, the wood of the grip smooth and cold against her fingers.

How many has he killed? The question came as she wrapped her fingers around the pistol and gently lifted it from the holster.

Too many. Came the answer as he tried to look away, to see what she was doing. She held his face with her free hand as the revolver came free.

"Do you want me?" She whispered, able to take a step back once the spell he'd held over her was broken She brought up the barrel of the pistol aiming at his stomach. He stopped, a cruel smile spreading across his lips as he shrugged.

"I'll shoot you," she said, aware that more than likely she wouldn't. She pulled back the hammer of the unwieldly weapon, the click loud in the stillness of the night. Her trigger finger pointed straight along the barrel as she had been taught by her dad so many years before.

He followed her across the room as she backed away. The backs of her legs struck the side of the bed and she stopped. Instinctively she wrapped her finger around the trigger and squeezed.

The roar of the pistol was deafening in the small room and her ears rang. Instead of falling, as she expected, he slammed into her and drove her onto the bed.

No way I missed. The thought spun through her mind, the sound of running footsteps came from beyond the door. Jamie shouted, pounding on the door, before silence enveloped her. Cold hands caressed her flesh and she retreated from what was happening.

22

Jamie woke to a room filled with shadows. A shaft of pale moonlight painted a square on the floor between them. The bed where Penny slept lost in a deep gloom.

"Penny?" He pushed himself up and looked around the room, the darkness in the corners filled with memories from the past.

"Penny?" He said again, louder, swinging his feet out of bed to cross to where she was supposed to be sleeping. He found the sheets cold and empty and crossed to the door.

In the hallway the night was deep, and he moved down its length with his hands stretched out before him. A soft voice came from his right and he turned in that direction to blindly follow it to a closed door. He wrapped his hand around the knob and stopped. Did he really want to see what lay on the other side? He knew what happened to the Reverend's wife, what she'd done after the death of her daughter.

No, it was better to let some secrets remain undisturbed, and he stepped back from the door to continue down the hall. Ahead the door on the left stood open, allowing the light of the moon to reach the hall and offer some relief from the all-consuming darkness.

He spotted Penny at the other end of the hall, watching something at the bottom of the steps. Booted feet pounded up the stairs, one of their captors appeared and Penny backed away from him vanishing into the room. The man followed, closing the door behind him, and Jamie moved down the hallway suddenly afraid of what was about to happen.

A gunshot behind the door drove him forward as the sound of running feet came from below. He reached the door, pounding on it, calling for Penny as the others gathered around him and the world spun out of focus.

Jamie woke up astride his horse, sauntering through the forest. Penny was on a horse next to him, and at each point around them, one of their captors rode.

"Where are we going?" He said.

"I don't know," Penny replied, and he noted how strained her features appeared. Her once vibrant red hair had been dulled, fading to a shade lighter than it had been before.

"Was it a dream?"

She turned to look at him with a thousand-yard stare that caused old terrors to stir in his mind.

"It's not a dream," she said, "it's a nightmare."

23

Gregory and Billie-Bob knelt behind the low wall running along the edge of the roof. Each with a rifle butt resting against their shoulder. Eyes glued to the telescopic sight as the last of the morning mist was burned away by the rising sun.

Meat was anxious to get going, to get this over with and get out of Richmond. The memory of the waking dream he'd had was still fresh in his mind. He worried it might prove to be a sign of bad luck, an omen things weren't going to go as planned.

"Downtown is a mess," Gregory said. "I can see people moving about in a couple of the high rises."

"Any sign of the kids?" Window said.

Gregory shook his head as he continued to scan the city center that was a little more than a mile away. "We're not close enough yet."

"Do you see anyone who might be watching for us?"

"Nothing," Billie-Bob said.

The sound of the bullet slapping into the escarpment below Gregory sent them all scrambling for cover. It was followed by a report that faded into the distance like thunder.

"Where did that come from?" Meat hunkered down below the edge of the low wall around the perimeter of the roof.

"Hang on." Billie-Bob squirmed into a new position. Carefully, he lifted his head above the lip of the wall. Ducking back as a round slammed into the edge of the lip, pieces of old concrete dancing across the roof behind him.

"It's coming from below," Billie-Bob said.

"Keep 'em occupied." Window and Meat worked their way to the door leading to the stairwell. Behind the cover of the maintenance shed they got to their feet and Meat stood to one side of the door. His revolver drawn, he motioned for Window to open the door.

Meat came around low, his pistol held out in front of him. Window raced down the steps to the landing and established a cover point before Meat followed and pushed down the second flight to the landing where the door for the top floor was located.

Carefully, they opened the door onto a gloomy hallway. The doors to a couple of the apartments stood open, allowing some light to come through. Other than that, it was a dark and dangerous place.

They entered an apartment whose door stood and crossed to the windows. Most of the glass had been broken out, the result of the vandalism that swept across the city as emergency services were overwhelmed in the initial days of the awakening.

The wall below the window was stained black with mold, the carpet below swollen with moisture and covered by a fine layer of black mold that resembled a well-manicured lawn. With a rag covering his nose and mouth Meat crossed to the opening. Window followed suit.

In this new age, it was best to take every precaution possible.

They'd learned early in life the mold growing in many of the still standing buildings had an adverse effect on the health of anyone who ingested the spores, taking root in the victim's lungs and growing until they could no longer breathe. Lung rot, they called it. With only basic first aid and no proper medical facilities, the tiniest cut could prove fatal, and lung rot offered a slow, and quite painful death.

Staying in the shadows, Meat searched the area around the apartment building. Movement drew his attention to an open window in one of the vacant houses facing the building. As he watched, a young man leaned on the windowsill and sighted his rifle on the roof of the apartment building. He appeared to be alone.

"Stay here," Meat said as he pointed out the young man to Window. "Keep an eye on him. I'll be right back."

Meat returned with Gregory. While Billie-Bob entertained his would-be killer, Gregory stood in the shadows and sighted in on the sniper. The muzzle blast of the shot, confined within the small room, caused some of the plaster above their heads to fall from the ceiling.

A hole was exposed and from the black depths came the unmistakable squeaking of rodents. With no one to slow their spread, rodents had taken over the city and Meat shuddered at the idea of having spent the night on the roof of a building whose walls were full of rats.

"We need to get out of here." Meat turned to the door and vanished into the hallway.

24

With the threat extinguished, they gathered their gear and spilled out of the gloomy depths of the building into the sunlit parking lot. The house their would-be killer used was directly in front of them and they spread out as they approached the vacant structure. Reaching the wall, Meat released his pent-up breath. He'd been expecting someone to pop up in the window at any moment, catching him exposed. Nothing moved in the shadowy depths of the house as they rounded the corner to an open door.

Inside they found the body of the lone shooter. All he had with him was a nearly empty backpack with several loose rifle rounds rifle lying on the bottom. Along with three dog-eared paperbacks, the covers of which had long since fallen off, leaving grimy title pages in their place. *To Kill a Mockingbird* shared the pack with *The Catcher in the Rye*, and *Of Mice and Men*.

Meat slipped the books into his own pack. He'd never heard of them before and was looking forward to some quiet time spent reading something new. He sensed they were important to the shooter, who now lay dead in a pool of his own blood. Why else would he have kept them? They must have contained a message he found valuable enough to take up space in his pack, space better used for food.

Once they were back outside, Meat surveyed the group. They were road weary and the lack of sleep from keeping a constant watch was beginning to show in the dazed expressions returning his gaze. They'd have to take a break soon, get some real sleep, somewhere away from the constant tension of surviving. It would have to wait. A group of children lost in the city were hoping someone would save them.

"We'll have to keep away from the roads from now on. I'll continue to check for signs, we don't want to let them know we're coming. Once we get closer, we'll find a high spot and look for the kids," Meat said.

If they're still alive, he finished to himself. He had lost the sign left by the group when they entered the outskirts of the city, yet he kept pushing on in the only feasible direction, relying more on instinct than anything else.

It had been nearly ten days since they had been taken, and he wondered if they were still alive. The concept of weeks, months, and years had given way to the days in the season. Mondays no longer existed, nor did weekends, as the struggle to survive was an endless one. A once mighty industrialized culture that took two centuries to build had been reduced to an agrarian society in less than a decade.

They kept to backyards as they moved deeper into the city, jumping over those fences that remained as they pushed through the overgrowth. Crossing over weed-choked expanses that had once been immaculate lawns where weekend barbecues were once hosted.

Breaking through a tangled line of underbrush, they came out into a perfectly manicured lawn. It was so out of place amid all of the destruction they stopped in their tracks to stare with wonder at the sight they had found. In ordered formations on the lawn stood rows of short yard gnomes. Each one carried a pointed hat tilted at a jaunty angles, with rosy red cheeks above full white beards resting upon swollen bellies.

Several hundred tiny statues stood in regimented rows like soldiers at attention, ready at a moment's notice to move forward. Their shirts the colors of the rainbow ordered in groups of red, yellow, blue, and green. They covered the immaculate lawn from one side to the other.

On their right, a house stood at the edge of the stone patio bordering the lawn. On the patio several wrought iron chairs stood around a solitary table. Everything was clean and white as if it had been freshly painted. It looked like someone had recently been sitting in them and would return at any moment.

"I don't like this," Window said, and Meat nodded in agreement.

The windows of the house, while clean, stood dark and silent. There could be any number of people standing behind them, watching them as they stumbled out of the forest into this land of gnomes.

"We gotta keep moving." Meat pushed out across the lawn, carefully stepping around the formation closest to them. His head on a swivel, trying to keep an eye on the house, while at the same time remaining focused on where he was going.

Weaving among the ordered formations, they moved in single file. Halfway across the sea of gnomes Billie-Bob stumbled into a row of the small statues. One fell into the next in line with a soft clunk. Like a row of dominos, the gnomes got knocked off their feet, coming to rest in the grass as their neighbors responded in kind.

They finished crossing the yard in a dead run, excepting at any moment for the owner of the house to emerge and find one of his formations disturbed.

They ran through the trees, branches slapping at their faces, the oppressive heat of the forest weighing down upon them like a physical presence. Meat stumbled to a stop as the rest plowed into him from behind, driving him to the ground where he lay panting as the absurdity of the situation slowly settled into him.

He laughed at the sheer strangeness of that backyard, while at the same time, a gentle chill caressed his spine. It made no sense. Amid all the destruction that had befallen the world, why would someone put so much effort into caring for such a bizarre display?

"Can you believe that?" Billie-Bob said.

They panted as they bent over at the waist, hands on their knees to support them, sweat dripping from their faces.

"It was the strangest thing I've ever seen," Gregory said. "I mean, who would do such a thing?"

"A little unhinged," Window said.

"Unhinged, my ass, that's loony tunes crazy," Billie-Bob said.

Meat understood what might compel someone to do such a thing. He'd seen it in the past, especially among the older people whose worlds had been turned upside down by the awakening. Doing anything they could to cling to the old ways. One day, they had been going about their daily lives, working, living, and following the endless cycle leading all of them to only one outcome.

Overnight, they were fighting for their lives. The things around them they had so long taken for granted were no longer there. The lights no longer came on when one flipped the switch, the heat remained off when they adjusted the dial of their thermostat, and to add insult to injury, the world had become an increasingly dangerous place to survive.

Survival of the fittest became the law of the jungle as society crumbled. The laws that once protected all of them were discarded in the face of a relentless hunger. Hunger not only for food, but for the security that once offered an illusion of safety.

"We gotta keep going." Meat pushed himself to his feet and brushed off his clothes, checking to make sure nothing had fallen from his pack when he fell over. Each of them nodded in response and Meat pushed on through the dense forest as its secret voice whispered all around them.

Here and there they came upon pools, some filled with stagnant water over which clouds of mosquitoes buzzed, others empty with the skeletal remains of unfortunate animals trapped at the bottom, surrounded on all sides by sheer tiled walls. From everywhere around them came the persistent sound of life in sharp contrast to their own silence as they pushed ahead.

Breaking through a dense section of overgrowth, they came out into a section of the city that had burned to the ground. Piles of scorched rubble lay scattered across the blackened ground. In several spots, parts of the once standing structure stood as silent testament to the density of the population that once inhabited this section of the city. It was empty now, the living having fled, or perishing as a result of the awakening.

The rusting hulks of several automobiles sat in what had at one time been a roadway, the asphalt surface melting from the heat of the fire, the cars sinking into the morass to become locked forever in black asphalt matching the scorched ground. It was like a scene from another world, a desolate place located at the end of a perverse rainbow.

The burned-out section covered six city blocks, a rolling expanse of destruction with several walls offering some cover. Directly across from them, its white surface blackened by the smoke from the long-ago fire, stood a massive square building that had escaped the fire unscathed.

Heat waves danced in the distance, the sun having emerged from behind a bank of clouds, burning off the earlier haze as the temperature increased to a more summer like level.

"What do you think it is?" Window said as Meat scanned the face of the building with his binoculars. Two rows of square windows were spaced evenly across the side of the building. One at street level, the other near the roofline. They had entered the city of Richmond. Beyond the squat structure stood taller buildings reaching for the cloudless blue sky above.

"I don't know," Meat said, "we're about to find out."

As a group, they set out across the plain of destruction, cinders stirring at their feet as they trudged across the blackened scar. Here the heat of the sun was intensified by the black surface absorbing the warming rays to amplify them. Sweat ran down their brows, trickling down their backs, staining their already dirty clothing.

Shortly, they entered in the shadow of the building as they neared what appeared to be a set of glass doors leading inside. The glass had long since been knocked out, with shards of glass lying in a glittering pile in and out of the building. Meat ducked down and slipped under the metal bar bisecting the door. Once inside, he took a deep breath, a familiar scent tickling his nostrils, and excitement filed him when he recognized the smell.

25

After Meat and the others left, Einstein busied himself cleaning his guns, lost in his thoughts as Maria tidied the house. He was still smarting over Meat's revelation of the true nature of Bremo Bluff. He'd lived there his entire life and had never suspected a thing. The fact his mom and dad had been involved from the start, which could only mean they had played a part in establishing the policy about what to do with those who wanted to leave, left him wondering what else he had missed.

He understood how important it was they protect what they had. The community had grown larger over the years, boasting well over two thousand survivors, leaving him to wonder if it was still necessary. He wasn't familiar with what was going on beyond the fence, this trip being the furthest he'd ventured from the safety it afforded, surely the world had not become that dangerous.

Maria passed through, drawing him from his thoughts, and he watched as she worked. She was slim and attractive, and with the warmer weather, she had shed her jacket, revealing the filthy t-shirt she wore underneath. It was obvious she wasn't wearing a bra, as her nipples tented the fabric. A tear in the fabric under her left breast exposed a gentle curve of bare flesh.

She was unlike any of the girls he knew at the Bluff. They were open and straightforward about what they wanted. Security topping the list. Though he understood the inner workings of the turbines providing their power, a knowledge providing him certain privileges within the compound, yet he was still a kid.

Maria was the exact opposite of the girls at the Bluff. Carrying herself as he imagined a lady should, like his mother, with a hint of regal dignity about her.

Sensing his stare, she stopped what she was doing and turned to face him. He quickly dropped his gaze to the disassembled rifle on the table before him.

"Could you help me with something?" she said.

He looked up, his eyes dropping against his will to the twin points on the front of her t-shirt. He dragged his gaze away, forcing himself to look her in the eyes. "Sure, what do you need?"

"We have to bury her."

"Who?"

"My mom. We can't leave her in the basement. Could you help me please?"

"No problem." He laid down the rifle bolt and pushed himself to his feet.

As he stood in the shadowy basement, the flickering flame of a candle providing some illumination, something his father said came to him.

"In this world, as in the past, there will always be the haves and the have-nots."

His father's words whispered as he recalled that day. After another boring day tracing wiring diagrams, he was ready to escape the stuffy confines of his father's workshop. The sun was shining outside, the weather had grown warmer, and he wanted more than anything to get out there and enjoy it. His father insisted he wait until he was done.

"The power plant gives us electricity, it gives us running water, we are the haves. Beyond the fence live the have-nots. It doesn't

matter if they didn't plan properly or respond as they should have to a changing world, or even that everything happened before they were ready. The fact remains, we have what they want, so we must always be careful about what we share with strangers."

Einstein watched as Maria knelt down and caressed her mother's cheek. Long shadows danced against the wall in response to the flickering flame of the candle. Had they been in the Bluff, all he would have had to do was flip a switch to fill the room with light.

Was she a have not? The question intruded and Einstein pushed it away. Since that day he had viewed those beyond the fence as primitive savages living in the dark. Maria was the second survivor he'd met in as many days who had proven to be the opposite of what his father said. If his dad lied about that, what's to say he hadn't lied about a person's ability to leave?

Maria's mother's stomach had swollen from the gases of decomposition and a rank odor wafted up from her figure. After wrapping her body in several sheets stripped from her bed, they secured them with a rope. Einstein fashioned a harness, and together they pulled her mother's body up the steps and into the kitchen.

26

At the edge of what was once the backyard, Einstein dug a shallow grave in the rocky soil. Next to it was the one Maria and her mother interred her little brother, Jamie. The soil over his small grave had a sunken, abandoned look, the ground disturbed where his head would have been.

Where he dug his way out afterwards.

"We didn't know," she said. "We believed when he died, he would stay that way, but he didn't." She sniffled as she wiped away a tear.

Einstein was overwhelmed by a desire to protect Maria. She might have been a few years older than he, more mature by some standards, at that moment, she was like a little child lost. He returned to the task of digging and in time had opened a respectable hole into which they lowered her mother's wrapped body. After pushing the dirt back, he stood up, dusting his hands off on his pants.

"We should say something," she said.

"I not sure what to say." Einstein knew everyone had their own way of dealing with death. Having grown up in a protected environment, this was the first time he'd ever been this close to it. His entire life was spent behind the fence at the Bluff, with no first-hand knowledge of what happened in the early days of the awakening. "My mom used to tell me the Lord's prayer all the time, I've got it memorized."

"That would be nice."

As he recited the passages, the voice of the forest continued unabated, punctuating his words, a reminder that life would go on. She slipped her hand into his and a spark shot the length of his arm, rebounded from his shoulder, before settling in the unlikeliest of places.

"It'll never be the same, will it?" she said after he finished.

"What?"

"The world, like it used to be. My dad always talked about the way it was. How safe it used to be. How convenient. If you wanted to go somewhere, you got in your car and drove. If you were hungry, you stopped and got something to eat. If you were thirsty, you got something to drink. We'll never see that, will we?"

Einstein shrugged. He'd heard the stories as well, not only from his parents and the other older people who lived at the Bluff. "Not much we can do about it."

"Weren't you ever curious about the time before?"

"Of course, what good is it to worry over what could have been?"

"I'd like to flush a toilet and take a hot shower," she said.

"Come back to the Bluff with us and you can."

"You have running water?"

"And, toilets, and showers, and sinks and drinking fountains. The drinking water comes from the steam used to power the turbines, we filter it, of course, and it's rationed. We also get hot water from the turbines, unfiltered. For everything else we use water from the river."

"What else do you have there?"

"We have electricity from the power plant, gardens, and many of us raise rabbits. Everyone who lives at the Bluff has a job to do. We pitch in to help one another. There's a big fence with guard towers that keep anything bad from getting in." *And those who want to leave from getting out*, he finished silently to himself.

"Sounds like a prison."

Einstein shrugged. He'd read about prisons at the Widow Winslow's little library, and one story in particular stood out in his mind. By a writer who was dead now, about an innocent man, a movie poster, and a corrupt warden. He couldn't remember the title, though he liked that in the end the innocent man got his revenge.

"I'm getting hungry, what about you?" Maria said.

Einstein nodded and she led him by the hand back to the house.

27

Throughout his short life, he'd been focused on one thing and one thing only—learning as much as he could about the inner workings of the power plant at Bremo Bluff, driven by his father who worked at the plant long before the awakening. While others his age were learning to read at the Widow Winslow's small library, he was poring over technical manuals detailing the mysteries of turning motion into electricity. As his peers followed the amorous adventures of gumshoe detectives, he traced complex circuit diagrams to isolate problems.

You have to know how things work in order to survive. His father's words drove him ever forward in his quest for knowledge.

His childhood had been an endless routine of taking things apart and putting them back together again. Learning the intricate secrets of the machines that once made modern man's life one of leisure. Like the tinkerers of the old west, he and his father amassed a wealth of knowledge about fixing broken machinery. He understood how to build a machine to perform multiple small tasks driven by a single electrical motor running in one direction.

Those who know how to make the machines work will be the ones who rebuild this world. His father was always fond of saying. Only he didn't want to be the one who built the machines. He wanted to travel beyond the fence, explore the world, rediscover the places lost to history.

Through all his lessons, he'd failed to learn the most important one. How to interact with the people around him, especially members of the opposite sex. As Maria fixed dinner, he watched silently, responding to her requests, answering her questions as she chattered aimlessly while she went about the business of fixing them a quick meal. There was so much he wanted to say, only he wasn't sure how to begin.

After dinner, as the sun sank behind the western horizon, she sat beside him on the back stoop, watching the evening darken to night. Stars twinkled in the sky above, the lack of light pollution revealing a glittering array of sparkling points of light that appeared to stretch beyond forever.

He wasn't sure what to do, so he slowly reached out with his left arm and carefully placed it across her shoulders. He waited to see what her reaction might be, surprised and pleased when she leaned against his body, and snuggled closer to his chest.

"It so beautiful," she said as she gazed up at the stars spread across the sky like jewels across velvet.

"Yep." He wasn't sure what came next, his left hand hung uselessly over her breast. He let it settle against the fabric of her shirt, an electric shock of anticipation, lust, and a high giddiness all mingling together as it traveled the length of his arm and spread throughout his body. She responded, her nipple stiffening under the fabric, and he gently squeezed as her hand fell to his thigh, a hot point against his chilled flesh.

The purple-headed bastard stirred, trapped between the fabric of his pants and his inner thigh, with nowhere else to go but along his thigh, to her hand. As her fingers lightly caressed that throbbing flesh, she looked up. Starlight glittered in her eyes, the cosmos reflected in her gaze.

Her breath was rancid, as was his, so it didn't matter. They kissed, long and deep, teeth clashing as their tongues probed one another. They tore at each other's clothes, buttons popping. Their breath ragged gasps as they sought each other's flesh.

He kicked off his boots, each one clumping down the steps abandoned as she struggled with his belt, her young breasts dancing in time with her movements, her nipples hard, softly illuminated by the moon as it rode across the night sky. Together they stood up and stripped off their pants, leaving them on the floor with the rest of their discarded clothing.

Now nude, they wrapped their arms around one another, the hot points of her nipples pressing against his chest. They kissed long and deep, hands probing each other's bodies, his member trapped against her thigh. She reached down and slipped him between her legs. She was moist. She wanted it as bad as he.

"If you catch me, you can have me," she whispered, her hot breath tickling the flesh of his ear.

She stepped back, turned, and ran down the steps to vanish into the forest that was once the backyard. Einstein followed as she weaved in and out of the trees, darting left and right, a faint smudge in the deep shadows. He caught up with her, or she let him, not that it really mattered. He wrapped his arms around her waist as she giggled, and he lifted her from her feet. Carefully, he lowered her to the moss-covered ground.

28

Einstein lay half asleep, adrift in that tranquil world between the reality of full consciousness and the comforting embrace of a dream that existed only in his mind. Rolling to his side, he reached out, expecting to find Maria beside him, his fingers coming into contact with the cold sheets they'd wrapped about them after a night of pleasure. He remembered the first time, each of them filled with a driving need that pushed aside all others, their hormones out of control as they struggled to meld their bodies into one.

It had been over in a flash, that uncontrollable urge washing through him as he slipped into that moist secret place. The memory awakened a stirring in his loins as he searched the sheets for Maria's warmth.

She's gone. He sat up, blinking in response to the sunlight streaming through the windows. Pushing himself to his feet, he slipped on his pants and moved through the house in search of her. He found her in the living room, fully dressed, packing a bag.

"What's wrong?" he said. "Where are you going?"

"I can't stay here anymore. I have to go. I can't believe what we did last night."

Einstein was bewildered by this sudden turn of events. He wanted to grab her and shake some sense into her, yet he kept his distance. A change had come over her and he was no longer certain he was a part of her life.

She was frightened, fear burning in her eyes.

What is she afraid of?

"What's wrong?"

She stopped, letting the last of her things fall to the floor. From outside came the sound of the birds in the trees around the house. Confirmation that no matter what happened, the world would continue on its predetermined course, that man for all his bravado, was not the supreme being he believed himself to be.

"What if I'm pregnant?" she said.

"What if you are? You can come back to The Bluffs with us, it's safe there."

"For how long? Aren't we kidding ourselves that everything is all right? That the world will continue to belong to us? And what kind of a world would we be bringing our child into? Is it fair to take their childhood away from them like that?"

"Look, I don't have the answers to everything." Einstein took another step closer, his hands held out in a questioning manner. "I do know that if we give up, it will all be lost. We have to keep fighting."

"What if I don't want to?"

"Who's to say you're even pregnant?" He was going to grab her, tie her up if need be, until she came to her senses. For every step he took, she took another back, keeping her distance.

"I know I am. I know it. It happened to my mom when she first met my dad. She told me not to ever do that, that I would get pregnant the first time, and this was no world to raise a child in."

"Come on, Maria, let's sit down and talk about this. Because it happened to your mom doesn't mean it will happen to you." Einstein leaned forward, reaching out with his hand, wrapping his fingers around her elbow.

"Don't touch me," she shouted as she yanked her arm away. She snatched her bag from the couch and darted out the front door. Einstein followed, still not dressed, his feet getting wet in the grass as he followed her around the side of the house and into the forest that was once the backyard.

"Where are you going?"

"I don't know, and I don't care. I gotta get away."

"Let me come with you?"

"No, stay away from me. I wish I would never have met any of you." She turned and stalked into the forest depths. Einstein ran back to the house and finished dressing. Leaving his pack and his weapons, he ran into the forest to catch up with Maria.

Branches slapped him across the face as he ran, and he struggled to keep Maria in view. He slipped and slid over the blanket of dead leaves that carpeted the forest floor, tripping over errant roots that snatched at his feet at will. The heels of his palms were scraped and bleeding from catching himself several times.

He was sweating profusely, the smell of his unwashed body rising up from his clothes was enough to make his empty stomach perform several lazy somersaults. Thirst burned in his throat, his tongue was swollen and stuck to the roof of his mouth as he drew in one ragged breath after the next. He became an automaton focused on one goal, catching up with Maria and making everything right. Around him the forest was teeming with life, that incessant chatter masking the sounds of what lay ahead.

Reaching a tree line bordering a paved parking lot, he stopped as a large building housing what was once a grocery store loomed into view. Maria stood transfixed by the sheer size of the building. More buildings stood to the right of the grocery store, the gaping maws of their front windows, the glass long since broken by passing vandals, gazing out upon the debris-strewn parking lot.

Several cars stood abandoned in their parking slots, their windows broken out, their once gleaming paint oxidized by the relentless sun, their tires flattened. In several, the remains of the hapless occupants sat withered and decayed behind plastic steering wheels, trapped for eternity in a traffic jam of the dead.

Voices came from the opposite side of the grocery store, and as Einstein caught up with Maria, he tried to pull her back to the safety of the forest. With a shout of anger, she yanked her arm from Einstein's grasp. Her shout alerted those on the other side of the grocery store and Einstein watched in dismay as several older men ran around the corner of the building, carrying rifles at the ready, shouting for them to stay put.

He reached for his revolver, filled with despair when he realized he'd left it at the house along with his pack and rifle. He had not expected any of this to happen and, as the men approached, he realized they might not survive this encounter.

29

Awareness came to Einstein in stages, beginning with the throbbing at the base of his skull. It spread outward, keeping time with the beat of his heart as pins and needles danced across the flesh of his right arm. He couldn't move his hand. It was trapped between his body and a chilled surface. As understanding grew, he became aware of his cheek resting against a hard, cold, surface. Its chill seeping into his jaw to leave the bone aching.

He'd been trying to protect someone. Yet he couldn't recall the details of what happened before unconsciousness claimed him. The memory was fuzzy, he recalled some bad men had been coming for them, and he clearly remembered being concerned about someone other than himself.

Who? The memories teased, fading in and out of focus as his consciousness grew, taking on the aura of a dream forgotten almost immediately upon waking. He was lying on his stomach, his head turned to one side. Opening his eyes, he was greeted with emptiness. He couldn't see a thing. He felt the floor beneath him, a cold steel surface, and he reached out to explore the world around him, afraid of what he might find.

Where am I?

His fingers found empty air as far as he could reach, finding nothing except the cold, featureless surface on which he lay He pushed himself to his hands and knees, his head throbbing in response as sparks ignited behind his closed eyes. A groan escaped him as he crawled forward until the crown of his head came to rest against another cold surface.

Am I blind?

An impenetrable emptiness lay around him. It contained no light, nothing to see by, and he reached out to steady himself against the wall as he slowly climbed to his feet. He rested his throbbing forehead against a cool, pebbly, surface. His breath left a spot of condensation and he licked it greedily to slake his thirst.

Muffled shouts came from the other side of the wall, a woman screamed, breaching the dam holding his memories at bay. He remembered how she looked, how she felt, her bare flesh hot against his own as they rutted like a couple of rabbits. With the morning she ran away, afraid she might be pregnant, and he followed.

Maria? What are they doing to her?

The voices came closer, rough men speaking in harsh tones. The sound of a slap, flesh against flesh, and someone whimpered. Rage washed through him, blotting out the pain, and as the sound of a door opening came from his left, he crouched, ready to leap forward and attack whoever was opening his prison.

Light outlined the rectangular shape of a door, it grew wider, spilling into the darkness shrouding him. Blinding him. He put up his hands up to protect his eyes as daggers of pain lanced into each. He recognized Maria's voice as she cried out, felt her stumble against his crouched figure, and he reached out to steady her, his hands coming in contact with bare flesh.

She wrapped her arms around him, pressing her body close to his, the smell of excrement, and blood rising up from her as the door swung closed.

"Don't you worry, boy, your turn's coming. A couple of the guys are looking forward to busting that young ass of yours." A harsh voice came as the light vanished, and the door slammed shut. Laughter punctuated the comment, drifting away as silence filled the darkness around them.

"Are you all right?"

She shivered in his arms, clinging to his neck, and he leaned back to rest against the wall, stretching out his legs so Maria could lie against his body instead of the cold floor.

"They hurt me," she whispered. "I think I'm bleeding inside. I'm scared, I don't want to die."

"It'll be okay," he said with a soothing voice, one hand caressing her head as he held her around the shoulder with the other. Something hot and wet soaked into his pants where she was sitting, and the smell of blood grew even stronger.

Why didn't I bring my guns? he worried to himself. If he'd brought his guns, none of this would be happening now. He would have killed their tormentors, or they would have died trying. Other worries arose, piling one atop the other.

How will the others find us?

Will they even look?

Meat might look for them. What about Window? They'd had their differences. Would Meat be able to handle these people on his own?

He was getting ahead of himself. If they made it back from Richmond, if they came looking for them, if they were successful. A lot of ifs were slowly piling up against them as a more chilling thought stirred.

How much longer will Maria be able to hold on? Based on the amount of blood even now soaking into his pants, how long would she survive?

And when she passed? What then? She still had the virus, all of them did, and without precautions after her death, she'd come after him.

He shivered, imagining himself trapped in a dark steel room with a zombie who would stop at nothing to eat him.

How could I hurt her?

She whimpered in his lap and he pulled her close, wrapping both arms around her body as he tried to keep her warm, and waited for what was going to happen next.

He now understood the world was a savage place as the survivors struggled to live. Filled with the haves, and the have-nots. The paradigm had shifted. He and Maria had become the have-nots, held captive by the haves. Their captors had freedom, the guns, and the power.

When their captors came for him. If they let him out of this place, he was going to do everything in his power to destroy them or die trying.

It was the only hope left to cling to.

30

Meat remembered the smell. It reminded him of the room in the Widow Winslow's house, the one filled with shelves crammed full of books. It was the unique scent of decay present in every library in the world.

The pages of a book are made of wood pulp susceptible to decay. Old books especially were prone to decay, leaving the pages brittle enough to fall apart when you touched them. This decay was responsible for the smell known in libraries around the world. Libraries Meat had heard about but had never seen.

As the others followed him into the building, Meat stood and breathed deeply of the scent. Other odors mingled with it, the most prominent being mildew, and a charred, burnt scent from the fire.

At the end of a short hallway, the room opened into a wide-open space with racks of bookshelves marching away into the darkness. The spines created a patchwork image of various colors. The second floor was a balcony running along the three outer walls. The front of the building had at one time been all glass. Now it was open to the elements, the metal frames that once held the glass in place was all that remained.

A massive circular desk stood in the center of the first floor. Here librarians once worked. Its surface, along with everything else covered by a thick layer of dust. In one chair, the skeletal remains of a librarian, who died at her post, sat as if she was waiting for a visitor to ask directions, or check out their latest find.

Meat ran into the depths of the library, pounding up the steps to the second level, where he raced from one shelf to the next. Taking down a book, he held it reverently in his hands staring at a cover featuring a western gunslinger with a crow perched upon his shoulder, a dark tower in the distance behind him. Carefully he opened the cover. The pages crackled as the book opened, fluttering in response to an unfelt breeze, the edges flaking away to fall to the floor at his feet. The center of the page remained, holding itself together briefly before it too crumbled away. The pages behind the first followed suit, forming a small pile at Meat's feet as disappointment flooded him.

A soft breeze stirred what remained of the pages and he looked up at the empty windows that once protected the contents of the library from the elements. The blinders had fallen from his eyes and he saw the library as it really was, not as he hoped it would be. Meat moved from shelf to shelf, his actions becoming more hurried as he found one after another book was no more than dust.

Meat moved to the next rack and pulled down a book, only to have it crumble in his hand. Everything lay at his feet—mankind's hopes and dreams, his knowledge of the world, and the recounting of his past had all turned to dust. It was as if man never existed, no more than a fanciful dream cooked up by a twisted god who loved a good practical joke.

"How will we learn?" Meat gazed at the pile of crumbled pages. A soft breeze blew through one of the shattered windows, stirring the pile of dust at his feet, and he kicked it before he turned and stalked across the balcony to the stairs.

When he first looked at it from the forest, he believed the windows were intact. They weren't, and everything inside was open to the elements. The heat of the fire had shattered the windows along the west wall. The rest had fallen prey to passing vandals who didn't deserve the world they inherited.

31

While Meat searched the shelves, Window, Billie-Bob, and Gregory used the opportunity to relax as best they could in several of the molded plastic chairs next to the central desk. Billie-Bob kept glancing at the dead librarian leaning against the counter.

"I wonder what it was like?" Billie-Bob said.

"What?"

"Life before all this happened, can you imagine a fast food place on every street corner? Supermarkets full of food."

"Is that all you think about? Food?"

"Don't you?"

"I think about a lot of things." Window shrugged. Since his confession to Meat, he'd found himself wondering what it might have been like if the awakening had not happened. Instead of being worried about food like Billie-Bob, Window was interested in cars. A couple of cars at the Bluff were used to transport workers to the coalfield suppling the power plant. They also had a train they used to transfer coal downriver.

The cars ran on the alcohol produced from wood in a contraption called a gasifier. It heated the wood, forcing it to sweat a form of glycol. One of the old timers told him it was the same process the Germans used to fuel their cars during World War Two. A conflict that was ancient history to Windows way of thinking, though it happened less than a hundred years ago. The barge operated on bio-diesel made from the field grass found everywhere.

All Roads Lead to Terror

He knew some things would never return to normal, and he was happy. From what he'd been told of the world before the awakening, he understood not everything was as rosy as many wanted to believe. Crime, overcrowding, and a sinking economy sapped the hopes and dreams of many who once lived in the area.

Wild Bill worked in the metal shop at the Bluff, a friend of the family who took Window in when he first arrived. Wild Bill took Window under his wing and told him the unvarnished truth about what it was like before the awakening. The rampant unemployment, home foreclosures, and bankruptcies seriously weakening the economy. He called it the loss of the American Dream.

To his way of thinking, the awakening was a godsend. It thinned the population considerably, forcing the survivors to work harder in order to survive in this new reality. Gone were the cell phones and computers spewing a constant stream of garbage taking away man's desire to survive.

On the balcony above his head, Meat moved from rack to rack.

"He acts like he's never seen a book before," Billie-Bob said.

Window shrugged. He knew what Meat was looking for. It was the same thing all of them sought. Maybe not exactly, but pretty damned close.

32

They didn't deserve this place, none of them did, and with a murderous rage burning in the pit of his stomach, Meat reached the bottom of the steps and crossed to where the others waited.

"Come on, let's get ready to go."

"We just got here," Billie-Bob said.

"Just do it, Billie-Bob" Window watched Meat closely. "We're gonna do it, aren't we?"

Meat nodded as he gathered up his things. Years ago, he'd read a science fiction story about robots called berserkers, and how they had been programmed with a single-mindedness focused on killing humans. It was how he felt at the moment—cold, emotionless, ready to destroy those who destroyed the history of the world.

They who ignore history are doomed to repeat it. His father's words whispered in his mind. As he walked across the main lobby to the front doors, for the first time he understood what those words meant. Without history to guide them, they would make the same mistakes as civilization struggled to rebound from the brink of extinction.

Shouts came from beyond the door and each of them instinctively faded into the shadows as the sound of running feet came from outside, growing louder as they got closer. A young child darted into the interior of the library, panting and scared. He raced towards the desk at the center of the room, stood for a moment as his head swiveled back and forth. He looked like he was looking for a place to hide. Approaching footsteps drove him behind the librarian's desk. He vanished as two older boys cautiously entered the building.

Meat watched quietly from one side, safely hidden by the gloom, his hand resting on the butt of his pistol. He spotted Window on the other side of the main entrance across from him, his revolver in his hand as the older boys searched through the debris for the child. The fourth hung back, watching the others.

"Come out, ya little bastard," one of the boys said.

"Yeah, we ain't gonna hurt ya, we just want to ask ya a couple of questions." The second boy cautiously crept around the side of the circular desk the child hid behind.

"I don't see 'em," the first older child said.

"He's in here, shitting himself, I can smell him. Keep looking. If we don't bring him back, Wasta will have our hides." A third boy stepped into the library from the bright street. He blinked several times as his eyes adjusted to the gloomy interior. He turned his head and was looking right at Meat. Their eyes locked and Meat caught the spark of recognition in the other's gaze before it drifted down to the pistol at Meat's side.

The boy was about to say something when Meat brought up his pistol and fired a single shot. It was a quick snapshot from the hip, yet his aim remained true, and a bloody red spot appeared in the center of the boy's forehead as his head whipped back from the impact of the round.

Pandemonium erupted as the two older boys, now trapped in a deadly three-way crossfire, raced around in search of a way to escape. The sound of Window's .44 hammered against Meat's eardrums as one of the boys spun around violently, the expanding round nearly taking his shoulder off in a spray of blood and bone.

The third boy fared no better. Trapped between Meat and Gregory, his body jerked first one way then the other as intersecting rounds slammed into his body.

As fast as it began, it was over and as the smoke from their weapons drifted above their heads, the fourth boy outside fled down the street. Grabbing his rifle, Gregory stepped outside and sighted down his scope. Meat had no idea how far the boy had gotten, and he watched as Gregory steadied the rifle before gently caressing the trigger. The rifle bucked in his hands, yet he kept his eye glued to the eyepiece of the scope, riding the recoil as he steadied the muzzle to fire again if need be. Apparently, it wasn't needed as Gregory lowered his rifle and stood for a moment, staring down the street.

Stepping around the counter, they found the boy who had been wounded by Window. He lay sprawled on his back, sweating profusely, his hand clamped over his shoulder as blood spurted from between his fingers. He wore a loincloth similar to the one the child at the barn had been wearing, and his flesh was covered by an array of strange tattoos. When he grimaced, they could see his teeth had been filed down to points.

"Where are the kids you took from Bremo Bluff?" Meat hunkered down next to the boy.

"Fuck you," the boy said.

Meat slapped him across the face, jogging his head to the side. "I'm about done with the whole lot of you. Where are they?"

His only response was a snarling glare. Window stepped over and placed the toe of his boot on the boy's injured shoulder, slowly increasing the pressure as the boy screamed and squirmed beneath them.

"He ain't gonna last much longer." Meat noted the darkness of the blood issuing from between the boy's fingers. It was arterial blood, he would soon pass out from loss of blood, dying shortly after as his heart struggled to maintain pressure in a shattered body.

"I know where they are." A young voice came from the shadows beneath the receptionist desk.

"Shut up," the older boy snarled weakly, his struggles diminishing as his lifeblood pumped from between his fingers.

Billie-Bob approached the dying boy, whispering softly as he knelt down and watched him. "And when he came to the place where the wild things are, they roared their terrible roars and gnashed their terrible teeth and rolled their terrible eyes and showed their terrible claws."

"Please," the boy whispered weakly, his eyes rolling up into his head, his foot shaking gently before becoming still. Billie-Bob closed his eyelids and retreated into the shadows as he whispered, "they roared their terrible roars, and gnashed their terrible teeth, and rolled their terrible eyes, and showed their terrible claws."

"It's okay, it's safe now." Meat coaxed the young boy out of the shadows.

He was much younger and looked like he didn't belong to the tribe, or cult, who kidnapped the children. He wore a torn and dirty pair of pants below a filthy t-shirt, at one time it had probably been white. He didn't have the rough edges common to other survivors. His hair was long but had once been trimmed.

"What's your name?"

"Tanner. What's yours?"

"Meat," he said, smiling in an attempt to put the boy at ease. He nodded to the others. "That's Window, Billie-Bob, and Gregory.

We're not gonna hurt you. I promise" As each of their names was mentioned they waved.

"Where are you from?"

The boy shrugged. "I don't know, they took me from my parents during the winter."

"They've taken other kids?"

"There used to be a bunch of us, but a lot of them decided to stay."

"Stay where?" Meat asked.

"They became a part of the path to heaven, love is pain, and pain is love. I think they were forced to stay."

Why are they kidnapping children?"

"To feed Wasta."

"What's a Wasta?"

The boy shuddered, frightened by the memory. "I don't know, when I first got there, they put me in the same room with him."

"Is it a man?"

The boy shook his head. "At one time maybe, now he's Wasta."

"What does he look like?"

"I don't know, it was always dark when they put me in there."

"You've been in more than once?"

The boy shook his head, his bottom lip trembling as tears welled up in his eyes. "Please don't put me back in there. I'll do anything you want, please don't put me back with Wasta."

"Do you know where they keep their prisoners?"

"I escaped from there, it's why they were after me."

"Can you show us?"

"I don't know, I don't want to go back."

"We won't let anything bad happen to you. I promise, we can protect you."

"I don't know." The boy turned as if he was about to walk away, glancing from the street to Meat, and back again.

"We can help you find your parents." Meats words stopped him, and he looked back at Meat.

"Nobody can find my parents. They probably don't even care about me anymore."

"I can help you find them. I promise." His only hope of finding the missing children was about to walk out the door. He couldn't let him go, not without a fight. He glanced at the others, surprised by their expressions. Gregory was shaking his head.

"We can find them." Didn't they understand how close they were?

"I hope you've got a mouse in your pocket." Window turned to the door. Billie-Bob picked up his pack to follow. Tanner crossed to him and placed his hand in Meat's.

"You promise to help me find my parents?"

"I promise, you show me where those kids are, and I'll help you find them."

"You won't let them hurt me?"

"Of course not, you have my word."

"I'll show you." Tanner turned and walked out of the library. On the street he stopped and motioned for the others to follow.

"Are you crazy?" Window stepped in close, "making a promise like that? How are we gonna find his parents?"

"I'll find them. But first he takes us to the kids. You guys take the kids back to the Bluffs. I'll help Tanner find his parents."

"I'm not leaving you out here by yourself."

"Then I guess you'll have to come with me."

"You bastard. You knew I wouldn't leave you."

"I have nowhere else to go," Gregory said, stepping into the ring.

"I ain't letting you guys go without me," Billie-Bob said.

"Then how will we get them home?" Meat asked.

"Let's find them first, then we'll worry about the rest. One step at a time." Window slung his pack over his shoulder and turned to the door.

"But you owe me," Window said before he stepped out of the library.

Meat owed all of them, more than they realized. He'd lost their sign at the edge of town, and now they were being led to them. It all seemed too pat, too convenient. He'd have to keep an eye on Tanner, make sure he wasn't playing them for fools

With a last glance at the ruined library, he followed. One day he would find a library still intact, the books inside impatient to share the secrets they held.

33

Wind whistled between the buildings as Meat and the others followed Tanner, weaving through a traffic jam of rusting cars clogging a debris-strewn street, abandoned where they stopped by those fleeing the city. Many of the initial survivors did not make it, trapped behind steel and glass, stripped clean by scavengers drawn by easy pickings, who converged on the city in the early days. The area had not been cleaned since, a promising sign that not many survivors remained in the city.

In the Bluffs in the early days, those who perished during the awakening were dealt with properly. Riggs was one of the old timers involved and with the proper bribe, a bottle of Barkley's brew. A homemade beer brewed and bottled by Randall Barkley. He was willing to share even goriest details. Including a few of the nastier mistake's others would sooner forget. A few of the tales involved members of the current council, and one past member who it was said, built a harem with a few of the less ugly undead women. It was no secret Riggs and the aforementioned council member rarely got along so most listeners ignored the drunken gossip. Chalking it up to sour grapes.

Here in the city the dead remained where they died, adding to the oppressive cloud hanging over the city. Serving as confirmation, as if any was really needed, the world had changed, and not for the better.

Garbage covered everything, papers plastered to asphalt by past rains, old clothes abandoned in the haste of flight, weathered, worn, like the world around them. It was the face of a dead city, yet its voice continued unabated, refusing to surrender to reality.

The impassive walls of the buildings had yet to surrender to Mother Nature, who was making steady progress in reclaiming what was once hers. Here and there spots of bright green testified to her tenaciousness. Flowers bloomed where concrete once prevailed, grass pushed up through cracked pavement, slender blades emerging from the detritus of a time whose reign had passed.

Perched atop the buildings on both sides of the street, watching their progress with beady black eyes, crows gathered in anticipation of their next meal. The pickings had grown slim in the city since those first days when blood flowed freely.

A commotion erupted over the remains of the boy Gregory shot as scavengers flocked to the scent of freshly spilled blood. With raucous cries, they swooped in, scattering those gathered over the body, stealing what they could before flying away. Nature's cleaners hard at work. In no time the body would be stripped to the bone.

Coming to an intersection, they stopped to look in each direction. As far they could see lay more destruction. In the distance, at the end of the street in the direction they headed, towering buildings loomed. It was the downtown area where massive skyscrapers created canyons of glass, steel and concrete. Around them the buildings stood no more than six stories tall.

The corner of the intersection on their right was occupied by an Enterprise rental business. Cars sat abandoned in the parking lot, their windows shattered, as were the windows in most of the buildings.

"How far is it?" Gregory said.

"Down the street, there's a tunnel we can use."

"A tunnel?" Window said.

Tanner nodded, pointing at a steel manhole cover in the center of the intersection before turning to resume his trek.

Meat's unease grew at the gesture. He'd been feeling unsettled all morning. The confrontation at the apartment building followed by the discovery of a bizarre display that did little to comfort him. Add to this his worry over the loss of their quarry's sign the day before, and the ease with which they found what they were looking for, all added to the deepening suspicions nagging him since they entered the city.

They're being led to the slaughter. With the sign gone, what choice did they have?

"Are you all right?" Window stopped next to Meat.

"I don't like it, it's too easy. I feel like we're being led into a trap." Meat's unease grew with the vocalization of his worries.

"They'll find they've bitten off more than they can chew," Window said.

Tanner continued on without them. When he was thirty yards away, he stopped and turned back to face them. "Are you coming? I told you I can show you the way in."

The four of them exchanged glances and Meat was comforted to see he wasn't alone in his worry. Their awareness of what might be coming would serve them well.

"Are we gonna keep going?" Billie-Bob carried a worried expression on his normally relaxed face.

"Yeah." Meat nodded. "Let's keep going." He surveyed the intersection where they stood.

Across from the Enterprise store stood a small corner diner. Over the empty maw of the front door, a sign hung from a single chain, turning slowly in a steady breeze accompanied by the scent of a dead city. Smoke and decay an ever-present stench.

Chef Mamusu's Africanne Café, the sign read. In the café, shrouded by shadows, the memory of a better time lay trapped in the dark wood décor. Soon the weather would do its damage and the once gleaming wood would decay, the memories locked within its depths lost forever.

Directly behind the corner building, built to fit within the space available, stood a drive thru for a local bank. The bulletproof window was still whole, though it showed signs of past attempts to shatter it.

A side door stood open and Meat wandered over to take a peek inside. He found a block of hundred-dollar bills wrapped in heavy plastic lying on the floor. Protected from the elements, they looked as fresh as the day they'd been printed. They wouldn't last. In time, even the plastic protecting the bills would surrender to the relentlessness of the elements, and the money inside, about as worthless as the paper it was printed on, would be returned to its natural state.

Their heads on a swivel, they moved down the street, weaving among the traffic jam of the dead, their weapons at the ready. This was enemy territory. They didn't know if anyone was watching from the vacant windows gazing out on the dead street. For Meat, it was the most uncomfortable sensation he'd known, surrounded by the evidence of a world that ceased to exist the day of his birth.

He was better suited to the forest. He understood its voice, the incessant sound of life whispering beneath the surface of his consciousness. In the city they heard only the restless voice of the wind, an occasional cry somewhere in the distance, and the chatter of the birds. To Meat, the city was an alien world and the sooner he escaped its confines, the happier he would be.

They came to a row of businesses, windows shattered, doors torn from hinges. It looked like a violent storm had recently passed down the street destroying everything in its path. Except for one section. Here, the glass in the single door was still intact, the drawn shade giving it the illusion the owner had stepped out and would be back any minute. On the white wall to the right of the door someone had written in heavy black paint.

HOPE!

Scattered around it, the solitary word was repeated in numerous languages, written by hand in black paint, all he believed proclaiming the same simple sentiment.

HOPE!

This simple message stood against all the violence washing through the city in the early days.

"What do you think it means?" Window said.

Meat shrugged, he couldn't help but smile. Like a beacon amid all the destruction, the message stood untouched, and the fact it survived filled him with a renewed optimism.

They would survive. All of them. The human race would overcome the despair now gripping it. In places like Bremo Bluff, and here amid all this destruction, hope would overcome the obstacles in their path. He rejoined the group, a spring in his step, comforted he was not alone in his desire to see the human race succeed.

His feeling of hope was short-lived as they came upon several corpses hanging from one of the few remaining streetlights. One of the corpses turned at the end of its rope and he recognized him as the young man who'd been kicked in the balls the day before while they watched from the roof of the apartment building. The other two were his friends, united in death, as in life.

"We're in their territory now," Tanner said as they stopped and gazed up at the hanging corpses.

"One hell of a way to mark a boundary," Gregory said.

"Where's the old man?" Billie-Bob said.

"Maybe he got away," Window said.

"Somehow I doubt it, keep an eye out," Meat said. "They probably know we're here."

Gregory checked his pistol. The others followed suit, preparing for the worst, while hoping for the best.

34

Reaching an intersection blocked by the snarl of an accident, Tanner dropped to his hands and knees. "This is as far as we can go. They'll be watching the street. We'll have to go under them."

Under them? Meat shuddered at the idea.

Tanner crossed to a manhole cover and motioned for the others to help him. After a brief struggle, Gregory and Window were able to lift the steel disc and they gently laid it on the street next to the hole.

As he watched them wrestle with the heavy steel cover, something occurred to Meat. *How did Tanner get out to begin with?*

He obviously didn't come this way, or the cover would have already been off. Down the street behind them he detected movement. Watching from between two wrecked cars he spotted several boys move among the abandoned vehicles crowding the street. They were too far away to see what they looked like.

He motioned for Billie-Bob and pointed down the street at the two boys. "Tell me what you see."

Billie-Bob sighted down his rifle, watching the two boys for a moment before he lowered his weapon.

"They look like the boy at the barn, and the ones in the library," Billie-Bob said. "Do you want me to take them out?"

"No, we don't want to alert them we're here if they don't already know it," Meat said, playing out the hand he'd been dealt. If they wanted to find the missing children, they'd have to allow themselves to be led to the slaughter.

"Are you coming?" Window said.

"We need to go down there?" A chill wound its way down Meat's spine as he gazed into the hole.

"What's wrong, are you afraid of the dark?"

"No, there's rats down there."

"Yeah, so, we're bigger than they are."

"And there's more of them than there are of us," Meat said

Tanner turned and climbed down the steel ladder, vanishing into the street. Carefully, the rest followed, one at a time, until they all stood in a square room twelve feet beneath the surface.

"Which way?" Gregory said.

Tanner turned and vanished into dense shadows.

"I don't know if this is such a good idea." Meat glanced at Window kept pace beside him.

"You promised you'd help him. Besides what choice do we have?"

"Not much I suppose, keep an eye on him, I don't want any surprises."

They reached a junction and followed Tanner who turned right. From the darkness around them came the unmistakable clatter of tiny feet on concrete.

Rats.

Meat looked left and right as they ventured deeper into the city. His imagination running wild, filling the gloom around them with masses of small furry bodies twisting and turning, slithering over and around one another as they kept pace with the small group invading their domain. His flesh crawled at the image of the rats washing over him in a wave of teeth and claws, ripping at his skin as they smothered him beneath their furry mass.

"It's ahead," Tanner said as they emerged from the darkness into a softly lit square similar to the ladder they used to enter from the street. He pointed at the steel ladder leading up. The rungs imbedded in the concrete of the wall. "It leads to the place where they keep their prisoners."

Gregory went first. He was the strongest and would be able to move the manhole cover to the side easier than any of the others. One by one, they emerged into a small room. A silent furnace in one corner, water pipes vanished into the walls, and steel ductwork ran across the ceiling above their heads. Everything was covered with a layer of rust, the result of years of neglect. It was a cramped space, hot and airless, and they were anxious to get out of its confines.

A single steel door offered access to the building. Once everyone was in place, they opened the door and slipped quietly into a narrow hallway. From the wall came the sound of children crying, distant shouts, and a steady pounding carried to them by way of the ductwork with wire mesh vents evenly spaced along one wall at their feet. The smell of unwashed bodies, of decay, of piss and shit, and cooking all mingled to create a greasy atmosphere lying heavy and bitter on the tongue.

"This is too easy," Window said. Meat nodded as he held his hand over his nose, breathing through his fingers, trying to filter the air with the scent of his own body.

"Stay back." Meat motioned for Billie-Bob to step back. The hallway spilled into a larger room. In the opposite corner, a wide set of stairs vanished into the upper levels.

Two young boys, armed with shotguns, emerged from the corner of the room. Muzzles aimed at the group, more came down the steps, flooding into the room. Some carried shotguns, others held knives, a few came armed with crude pikes fashioned from whatever was handy.

Meat raised his hands, Window and Gregory followed suit, each of them aware of the same thing. They were outnumbered, and though they were armed, it wouldn't do much good in the close confines of such a small room. Most likely they would end up killing themselves from ricochets. Looking around, Meat was comforted to see Billie-Bob was not with them.

"Pain is love, love is pain," the children said in a single voice. None of them appeared to be older than twelve. A taller boy, their leader, pushed through the crowd.

"Punish us for our trespasses, love us with steady hands, show us the path through our pain for pain is love, and love is pain," The taller boy said as the crowd parted for him. He was savage and lean, his dusty flesh covered by intricate tattoos, a full head taller than the others around him as the children repeated the passage. He wore a loincloth made from a set of drapes. His eyes held no fear, or anger, only an animal like savagery.

Reaching them, he waved his hand for silence and the children gathered behind him grew quiet. He looked each of them up and down, sniffing the air about them, a smile spreading across his acne scarred features.

"I told you I could bring them to you," Tanner said. "Now let me go like you promised."

The leader glanced at Tanner with an annoyed expression, revealing rotting teeth filed down to points. His exhaled breath carried a decaying scent that turned Meat's stomach.

While they might not have been paragons of dental hygiene, they managed to care for their own teeth to a point. With no real dentists available, their only option for a bad tooth was to have Harvey, one of the blacksmiths at the compound, yank out the offending object. Without anesthesia, it was an option that compelled many of them to take better care of themselves. The lack of processed foods containing refined sugar helped cut down on the number of cavities.

The leader motioned for two older boys who moved forward to flank Tanner.

"You promised I'd never have to go in the room again," Tanner said.

"You won't," the leader said.

"No," Tanner shouted as he tried to back away. The two older boys grabbed him by his arms. "You promised me!"

"Send him to Heaven," the leader said.

"No, not that, put me back in the room, please, you said I could be free."

"You will be free," the older boy said, his voice even, devoid of emotion. "You will ascend as all before have ascended to the gates of Heaven."

"No," Tanner screamed as he was dragged into the crowd.

"Send him to Heaven," the assembled boys shouted in one voice as Tanner was led away, the crowd parting before them like the waters of the ocean parting before a passing vessel. Tanner struggled against his captors, trying to break free, his eyes filled with terror.

Meat followed their progress, and as they reached the stairwell, he spotted the message painted on the wall above the steps.

This way to Heaven!

Drops of the red paint dripped down the wall beneath each letter, tracing lines like blood staining flesh.

This way to Heaven!

Meat shuddered at the message as the leader stood before him, his eyes locked with his own. He glanced to his left, breaking the contact, bowing for now to the whims of this savage. This was not the time or place to make a play. It was too confined, and there were too many of them. From the corner of his eye he watched as the leader sidestepped to stand in front of Window, who locked gazes with him.

Don't do it, Window. Meat watched the two as they stood toe-to-toe, staring into one another's unblinking gaze. Surprisingly, the leader was the first to blink and he took a step back, quickly recovering his composure before anyone noticed what happened.

"To the master." The leader tapped Window and Meat on their shoulder.

Stepping in front of Gregory, the leader looked up into the older man's face. Gregory refused to look away, his eyes burning with a murderous rage, his hands clenched at his sides. Unmoving as one of the children stepped forward and slipped the rifle from Gregory's shoulder, vanishing into the crowd with his prize.

These children murdered Gregory's wife and daughter and Meat was surprised by the restraint the man was showing.

"To Heaven." The leader tapped Gregory on the shoulder before he turned and walked away, the crowd parting as he passed through, closing behind him as the children gathered around their captives.

"To the master. Pain is love, love is pain," the young boys shouted in a single voice, their eyes alight with primal glee.

"To the master, pain is love, love is pain." They swarmed around Meat, Window, and Gregory like workers bee's intent on tending to the queen. Driving them to the steps where others waited.

"To the master. Pain is love, love is pain," the assembled children shouted as Meat, Window, and Gregory were driven up the stairs by the mass of bodies pressing in all around them. On the first landing, they turned to climb the next flight of stairs to discover the same message written on the wall above the rusting handrail.

This way to Heaven!

When the room was empty, Billie-Bob emerged from the hallway. He stood inside the door listening to the chanting of his friends' captors. He wasn't sure how he was going to pull it off, he'd have to save the others, and do it quick.

They did have two advantages. The children had not taken any of their pistols, and they didn't know about Billie-Bob.

35

Meat and Window moved up the stairs surrounded by a sea of young boys. Voices echoed from the walls around them. A single name shouted like a chant.

"Wasta."

Who was this Wasta? What did he want with them?

Each landing was crowded with stacks of rotting garbage, buckets of waste, and discarded propane tanks. The smell overwhelmed Meat, making him gag as he struggled to breathe, the stench burning the back of his throat. The children remained oblivious to the smell.

This way to Heaven! Was written above each set of steps, an arrow beneath pointing to the shadowy stairwell above. Meat didn't understand what it meant. He suspected, based on the response from Tanner when the leader sent him to heaven, it couldn't be good.

Aside from the message black and white drawings covered the walls, some crude, others bordering on genius, with varying levels of ability and detail in between. Though unique in execution, they all featured a cross wrapped in barbed wire. The more detailed images included Christ nailed to the cross, or a person who represented their savior.

Around the images a single message was written in simple block letters or flowing script, as if each person who lived here needed to publicly proclaim their belief. Pain is love, and love is pain. Scattered among the drawings of the cross and the proclamations trinity triangles dotted the wall, three triangles intersecting one another.

On the wall above one flight of stairs, where it was difficult to reach, it looked like someone once disagreed with the belief exhibited by the children. Faded by the passage of time, someone wrote. Pain is hate. He smiled at the notion someone once opposed the leader. He doubted they still lived, at one time someone stood counter to their view.

As they climbed higher Meat realized he'd seen no girls. At each landing, he searched the hallways for any sign of the children they came to rescue. His hand never leaving the butt of the pistol in his waistband. Afraid if he let it go one of the boys would claim it. It surprised him no one took their weapons aside from Gregory's rifle. He was hesitant to draw attention to them and remind them of the danger they'd allowed into their midst.

On the fifth floor, after climbing ten flights of stairs, the group stopped. The group split, driving Meat and Window down the hall while Gregory and the remainder of the group vanished up the steps. Sunlight illuminated the message, casting a familiar shadow Meat studied it, trying to make sense of what it meant.

As the boys guided him and Window down the hallway, he recalled where he'd seen the image before. Open doors on both sides of the corridor offered some illumination, revealing a layer of garbage stretching the length of the hallway.

They knew about religion and belief systems, the power of the cross and what it represented. At the Bluffs every Sunday they held regular church services, more for the older generation than the young. Meat attended one of the services out of curiosity.

What he discovered was a stuffy belief with no room for the reality in which they lived. It offered little hope for the future, save an empty promise of life after death. Meat knew firsthand what life after death was like, and it was far from pretty.

As they neared the only closed door, he realized what the shadow on the wall looked like and a cold chill slithered the length of his spine. It looked like a cross with someone or something hanging from the upright. He began to understand the images he'd seen on the walls, and those tattooed to young bodies. Sometime in the past, someone introduced them to Christianity, in the interim they embellished their belief system to suit their own purposes, and those of this master Meat suspected he and Window was about to meet.

36

Let it play out, Gregory reminded himself as he was forced up the stairs away from Meat and Window. Coming to a landing, the first thing he noticed was the smell, the scent of death carried on a steady breeze through an open door leading to the roof. The second thing was the raucous cry of a crow accompanied by the sound of beating wings punctuated by the pain-filled cry of someone beyond his view.

As they rounded the bend in the stairs and the roof beyond the open door came into view, his earlier resolve crumbled, and he backed away with a strangled cry of terror as the children drove him towards the opening.

"No," he shouted as he turned to flee, and they pushed back as one. He was four times the size of the biggest boy, only size didn't matter when you faced a group as large as the one surrounding him.

In a blind panic, he drove himself into the group of boys, his meaty hands grasping at young flesh as he battered his way through them. Shouts of anger and pain surrounded him as the image of what he'd seen on the roof was permanently burned into his mind. They'd bastardized a belief he'd grown up with, turning the precept of religion on its head to satisfy their own savage desires.

They screamed around him in savage voices as he plowed into their midst, the steps only a few feet away as he battered and smashed his way through a wall of living flesh. Small fists rebounded from his face with little effect, panic blinding him to the pain as the boys around him fought to get his thrashing figure under control.

He was surrounded by shouts, screams and yells, an indistinguishable blur of noise as he focused all of his energy on one thing and one thing only. Reaching the steps and escaping. If he could reach the steps, he stood a good chance of getting out of this alive. His only alternative lay behind him, mocking him.

Knives flashed around him, cutting through the soft flesh of his arms and torso as the fight escalated, and like a raging bull, he pushed on through the boys. Swatting them out of his way, smashing with fists, driving them into the walls containing them. One of the boys fell over the railing with a scream dwindling into the dark depths of the building below. Several more fell down the steps, bones breaking on contact with unyielding concrete.

Something slammed into the back of his head, stars exploding behind his closed eyelids as he dropped to his knees, his hands outstretched with the top of the steps inches from his fingertips. The flesh of his bare arms was covered by a multitude of cuts, blood staining them, coating the floor with smears and swipes.

It was then, as he lay on the cold concrete, their bodies pressing down upon him, he remembered his pistol in the waistband of his pants. His panic blinded him to the fact he was still armed, and he plunged his hand down the front of his body, squeezing his arm between him, the concrete floor below, the weight of the pile of boys clinging to his back pressing him down.

He yanked his arm free, the pistol grasped in his hand, and fired wildly as the boys screamed with a savage bloodlust. The shots shook the air in the close confines of the landing, plaster falling from the ceiling and walls as the slugs passed through flesh, shattering bone, and sending several of the boys reeling into the shadows.

Blows rained down upon his head, bouncing his skull from the concrete, and with a final burst of strength he managed to lift himself and the pile of boys a few inches off the ground. It was too much for his body to bear and he dropped back to the pavement as the bleak emptiness of unconsciousness reached up to claim him.

37

While Meat and Window was being led to a closed door in a dark hallway, and Gregory was driven towards certain death, Billie-Bob crossed to the stairway. He stopped for a moment, reading the message on the wall written in dripping red paint bearing a resemblance to freshly spilled blood.

This way to Heaven!

With no idea what the writer's intent might have been, he knew on a primitive level, it wasn't good.

Eight steps led to a wide landing where eight more rose in the opposite direction to another landing. As he stood on the landing, he sensed the movement of a presence behind him. Glancing back into the depths from which he'd emerged, he spotted a darker object gliding across the room to the steps. Goosebumps danced across the flesh of his arms as the short hairs at the nape of his neck stood at attention.

Silence wrapped the basement in its grasp. The sounds of voices and shouts, of pounding feet racing up and down the steps above him, came as if from a great distance away.

Something's coming.

He raced up the steps to the next landing, afraid, yet unwilling to admit that whatever moved in the shadows below frightened him. Reaching a steel door, he slung his rifle across his back and pulled his pistol from the holster on his hip. Resting its barrel along his leg he carefully opened the door and peeked through the narrow crack.

On the other side of the door lay a garbage-strewn hallway. The overpowering stench of piss and shit was strong with an undercurrent of decay coming from the garbage covering the floor. Opening the door further, he peeked around the corner in the opposite direction. A window at the end offered some illumination. Seeing the hallway was empty, he stepped into the corridor, letting the door close softly behind him.

Closed doors lined each side of the hall, and next to each sat a five-gallon bucket which proved to be the source of the smell. Each one was half full of human waste. Mounds of paper discarded plastic bags, styrofoam plates, and the scattered bones of assorted small animals covered the floor. Beneath the surface of the garbage he detected movement as rodents foraged freely within the shaded recesses.

"They roared their terrible roars and gnashed their terrible teeth and rolled their terrible eyes and showed their terrible claws," Billie-Bob whispered as he surveyed the hallway. The walls between each door was covered with writing and drawings all in a heavy black marker. He recognized a drawing of a cross bound in barbed wire, wondering what the artist intended with such an odd combination.

Pain is love. Love is pain! Was written all around the images, in a variety of hands and inks, some resembled the rusty color or dried blood.

Pain is love. Love is pain? It made no sense. He was familiar with Christianity and what the cross meant. He and Meat went to a church service in the Bluffs once, and while Meat disliked the whole concept of life after death. Everyone knew what life after death meant in this new reality.

Billie-Bob found it difficult to place his trust in a supreme being who would allow the awakening to take place. He might work in mysterious ways, yet there was nothing mysterious about what happened. Others argued the awakening was the rapture written about in the bible. By then he'd heard enough.

Each of the four quadrants around the cross, bisected by the members of the cross, contained a smaller drawings of a double triangle. Drawn from one continuous line it created the illusion of three triangles wrapped around one another.

"They roared their terrible roars and gnashed their terrible teeth and rolled their terrible eyes and showed their terrible claws," he whispered as an old memory stirred at the sight of the triangle. He'd seen it before, not as a drawing, but as a piece of jewelry hanging from his uncle's neck.

The memory filled him with a sense of shame and self-loathing, coupled with a healthy dose of fear. He'd successfully blocked everything that happened during he and his brother's stay with his uncle. Now, with the all too familiar image all around him, the memory rose up from a dark abyss, freed from its prison.

Something stirred in the garbage at his feet, and he ignored it, transfixed by the image of the triangle. The memory of his mother abandoning him and his brother with his uncle whispered in his mind. He and Bobby was only four when she left them.

He only knew what he'd been told. She was ill equipped to care for them, unable to even care for herself in this new reality. When she was pregnant, she took refuge with an older man who protected them in the early days of his life. As with all things, they eventually changed, and her protector died in a firefight with a marauding band of survivors. She fled with her boys and all Billie-Bob could remember was a kaleidoscope of dark images as she found her way to her brother's where she left Billie and Bobbie.

As the old memories stirred, and a tear traced a wet path down his cheek, something touched his ankle. He looked down, at a slender appendage protruding from the garbage-strewn floor. Its flesh a mottled gray with black splotches in a random pattern along its length. It was firmly wrapped around his ankle, the tip probing the top of his boot as it sought entry into his pant leg. Luckily his pants leg was stuffed into his boot to prevent snakebites.

He lashed out, kicking the appendage away, backing across the hallway with a strangled cry. The slender tip swung back around, like a dog searching for its prey, tilting back as it sniffed the air. It dove in for his ankle and he sidestepped it, the tip slamming into the wall with a muted *thunk*, penetrating the surface of the plasterboard and becoming stuck in the drywall.

As it struggled to extract itself, its entire body shook, shedding the garbage camouflaging it. Exposing its entire length stretching down the hallway, vanishing into the darkness at the other end. The tip came free, whipping around as it unfurled its body.

Billie-Bob ducked and ran down the hallway. Reaching a foyer, he glanced back to see the tip of the appendage as racing towards him. It resembled an octopus' tentacle without the suction cups. The narrow tip was riding a muscular body folding over upon itself as it pursued him. Slithering like a massive snake through the garbage. Rats squealed as it passed through disturbing them. Pushing his way through a steel door, he stepped into a dark stairwell and leaned with his back against the door.

"What the hell was that?" he said, no response coming from the empty shadows around him. There'd been some strange stories in the past from the scavenging crews venturing beyond the fence, yet nothing could come close to explaining what he'd seen.

The tentacle drove into the door behind him, forcing it open slightly before it slammed shut under his weight. It struck the door again as Billie-Bob leaned into it.

A faint light came from somewhere above and, as his eyes adjusted to the gloom of the stairwell, he spotted a board leaning against the wall next to the door. Grabbing it, he propped it under the handle to block the door as the tentacle on the other side continued to pound against the door's face, dents appearing on his side of the metal door, attesting to the power of this creature's persistence.

He turned to face the black depths of the stairwell behind him. The steps going down led to an inky well, while the stairs above glowed with a faint light. Sensing movement below, he climbed the steps in the opposite direction, away from those bleak depths.

38

The boys shoved Meat, and Window into an airless dark room that smelled of musty despair, slamming the door behind them. The odor of unwashed bodies mingled with the old yet familiar scent of decay, beneath it all lay an oddly familiar sweet tang Meat struggled to identify. A narrow sliver of sunlight outlined the plywood covering the window, providing some illumination. As Meat's eyes adjusted to the gloom more details of their prison emerged. A small kitchen was on their right. A stove and refrigerator, next to a short counter. The sink was filled with old dishes, and a thick layer of dust covered everything.

To the left of the kitchen, where the tiled floor met dusty carpet was a sparsely furnished living room. A couch with two end tables and a coffee table sat grouped against one wall. Above the desk opposite the couch, a flat panel TV was mounted to the wall.

"How high are we?" Meat crossed to the window to inspect the plywood. It was securely fastened around the perimeter with what looked like hex head bolts. It would be a struggle to get one of them out without tools.

"I counted five floors as they brought us up." Window tried the door, glancing back at Meat when he found it unlocked. He opened the door and checked the dark corridor beyond. "What is it? he whispered.

"What? What did you say?"

"Nothing." Window closed the door and turned back to Meat. "What do we do now?"

"Get out, find the kids, and get away."

"They posted a couple of guards in the stairwell."

"Can we take em?" Meat pulled back the slide of his pistol, checking the load.

Window shrugged. "We don't have enough bullets for all of them. Where do you think they took Gregory?"

"To heaven, I guess." Meat recalled the shadow he'd seen on the wall at the bottom of the steps where they separated them. He hoped they could get out of this before it was too late. From the wall next to him came a steady scratching. The sound intensified, awakening an old memory, and with his mind's eye he found himself at a faded door at the end of a dark hallway.

"Do you hear that?" Meat said.

"What?' Window turned from the door.

"In the walls, scratching."

"Probably rats," Window said. "Why did they bring us here and leave? And who is the master?"

The scratching grew louder as the old memory surfaced, rising through the oily waters of a stagnant swamp.

"Maybe they're feeding us to whatever it is." Window stopped in front of Meat, looking at him with a worried expression. "Are you all right?"

"I guess, why?"

"You don't look so good."

"I feel okay."

"Are you sure?"

"I'm okay, quit worrying so much." Movement against the far wall caught Meat's eye. Floral wallpaper, red flowers against a white background, covered the walls. For a moment it looked like the wall rippled in response to movement beneath it. Like something moving beneath the surface of a perfectly still pond, disturbing the water's surface to mark its passage.

The object vanished into the narrow cracks around a closed door and Meat was overcome with a need to see what lay on the other side. The same need that once compelled him to open a similar door so many years before. From behind the door came the rustling sound of movement, the clatter of clawed feet upon a hard surface, the cry of a baby.

He crossed to the door, and stopped, his hand inches from the knob. Beyond waited a truth he'd struggled all his life to put behind him.

The baby's cry sent a chill down his spine and the years between then and now vanished. Once again, he was a child, hiding in an abandoned house with the man he called dad. Drawn to a closed door at the end of a long hallway on the second floor. The past and the present came together as he approached the door with hesitant steps. Soft light illuminated the narrow strip between the floor and the bottom of the door. A glow that pushed back the night and offered refuge from the terror throbbing with evil intent all around him.

It was like he was still trapped in that old house, forever bound to a single point of time. When he discovered what lay behind the door he screamed as only a terrified child could. The vocalization of his fear drawing the man he called dad. Pounding footsteps raced down the hallway. Rough hands grabbed him and pulled him from the room. Slamming the door on what he'd seen. It was too late and the image was burned into his mind, an image he'd never forget.

Pain is love, love is pain. He recalled the unforgiving way the man he once knew as his father pulled him from the room. An act of love that left an indelible scar.

Pain is love, love is pain.

Now, he faced the door again. This time, there would be no one to save him when he revealed the secret behind it. As he reached for the knob, he felt it all around him, a presence that was as much a part of the walls of the building as it was the air he breathed. It enveloped him in a chilled embrace, drawing him to the door with growing excitement, a wild abandon washing through him with barely restrained anticipation as his hand settled on the knob.

On the other side of the door lay a truth that would set him free and help him make sense of the world around him. As the door opened, from the darkness beyond came the sound of movement. Tiny claws dancing across a hard surface as the smell of decay washed out of the room, and the door swung open.

In the center of the floor, illuminated by a faint glow, stood a bassinet. In the shadows beneath it, the floor seethed like the surface of a storm-tossed ocean. Darker objects slithered over and around one another with the island of the bassinet in the center. The cover was up, concealing what lay within, yet Meat knew what waited for him on the other side of the innocuous white fabric.

Black things moved up and down the side of the crib. Tiny claws grasping for purchase against the material of the bassinette. Creating a distinct sound that served as a trigger for the memory filling his mind as he stepped around the side of the baby bed.

A single tear traced a dirty path down his cheek as the air around him filled with an expectant hush. From the bassinette came the cry of a wounded animal punctuated by the growl of a predator as it took its prize. Dark shapes continued to race up and down the sides of the bassinette, tiny claws tapping against the material, muted squeaks as teeth flashed like sparks.

Something stirred, reaching out across a vast gulf of time and space, curling itself about his psyche like a cold, strange, thing seeking warmth. It brushed against his cheek and for a moment, he was aware of some alien thing taking sustenance, not from the salty substance of the tear, but from the terror infusing it. A terror born one fall day when a five-year-old child discovered the truth about the reality in which he lived.

The memory of that day was unleashed, and as he stepped around the side of the bassinette, he was no longer the self-assured fourteen-year-old who led a band of his peers in search of the missing children. He became what he'd always been at heart. A frightened five-year-old trapped by terror.

Sitting in the bassinette, surrounded by a pile of decapitated rats, an infant looked up at him with silvered eyes reflecting the soft light. The baby had turned. In place of its once pink flesh was the pallid gray of a diseased carcass. Meat was unable to look away as the baby moved with a disjointed pantomime of life. It brought a squealing rat to its mouth and savagely bit off the head. Dropping the corpse onto the growing pile around while it chewed on its prize as pudgy hands sought another victim.

It was a tradeoff. The rats still alive fed on the exposed viscera lying in a pile in the baby's lap. Like a twisted parody of a Venus flytrap, the baby was using the scent of its ruptured abdomen to lure its victims to their doom. Unable to seek sustenance on its own, it adapted to the situation as best it could.

The inside the once white bassinette was darkened with blood and the baby looked at him with ravenous, cataract-coated eyes. It leaned forward, pushing aside the pile of carcasses, reaching for the side of the bassinette with pudgy, blood-covered hands while those sparkling eyes locked with Meat's face.

His tears flowed freely as an alien force surrounded him, embracing him with a chilled presence that sent goose bumps dancing across his flesh. Something licked his face as hot tears spilled down his cheeks. A rubbery coarse object pulled at his flesh as it dined on the terror feeding the tears.

Meat pulled his revolver as he backed across the room. Leveling the muzzle at the baby, he fired, the sound hammering his eardrums in the confines of the small room. Pounding footsteps came from beyond the opened door and Window raced into the room carrying a candle.

"What the hell, man? What are you shooting at?"

Meat looked back at the center of the room where the bassinette once stood. It was gone.

"Where did it go? It was right there." Meat pointed at the center of the floor where his shot hit, a stark white spot of exposed wood against the filthy surface of the floor.

"What are you shooting at?"

"Nothing." Meat holstered his pistol and shook his head, turning around in a slow circle.

In the faint light they spotted a murky figure standing against the wall to their right. Assorted drawings covered the walls around them, interspersed with a name written in thick black marker.

Watson, the oldest writing proclaimed, and upon closer inspection, the crude renderings of Celtic crosses wrapped in barbed wire surrounded by assorted passages from the Bible became clear. A single phrase repeated among them.

Pain is love, love is pain.

"I think I know who the master is," Window said from the other side of the room.

They built a shrine to honor him.

The mummified corpse of an older man was crucified on a rough wooden cross. A dirty white collar circled his throat. Barbed wire was wrapped around his outstretched arms and his body. Drawn tight, the barbs pierced the flesh, staining the fabric of the coat with spots of blood. In the center of each palm, a rusted nail protruded from rotting flesh. It was obvious he was alive when they crucified him, the nails had torn the flesh of his palms.

"Looks like they might have taken his teachings a little too seriously."

"Did they think he was a god?"

"Maybe."

The handle of a butcher's knife protruded from the man's right eye and Meat imagined the children huddled in the dark as their leader, whom they'd crucified, was reborn into a flesh-eating demon, fulfilling an ancient prophecy as it fed on their terror and the darkness in turn fed upon their fear. He had risen as their belief said he should, unfortunately what awakened on the cross bore little semblance to the man he once was.

Looking closer, Meat found a network of interlaced veins covering the leathery flesh of the dead man's face. The same type of veins covered his hands as well, vanishing beneath the cuff of the heavy black jacket he wore.

"What are you looking for?" Window said as Meat knelt and looked at the man's feet hanging several inches above the floor. From within the loose cuffs of his black pants, twisted strands of the veins ran to the floor, snaking away into the dense shadows, coming together in a thick strand of veins running along the wall behind the body, following the corner where the wall and floor met.

"Look at this," Meat said.

"What the hell is it?"

"I dunno." Meat removed his knife from the scabbard on his belt and probed the surface of the membrane. The flesh was elastic, giving as he applied pressure, bouncing back to its original shape when he released it.

Pushing harder, he penetrated the surface, and was rewarded with a thick yellow liquid oozing from the wound around the tip of his knife. A putrid stench rose from the liquid, reminding him of the pus from an infected wound.

"It's in the walls." Meat traced the object to the corner where it vanished behind the drywall.

"What's in the walls?" Window said as he watched over Meat's shoulder.

"I don't know what it is, all I know is I want to get out of here." Meat pushed himself to his feet and crossed to the door. After a quick glance down the hallway, he looked back at Window. "Are you ready?"

"It needs our terror to survive." Window's gaze was focused on something over Meat's shoulder. Meat swiveled his head around to search for what Window was looking at, finding emptiness behind him.

"Did I ever tell you I was afraid of spiders?" Window said.

"What are you talking about? We need to get out of here." Meat shook his head as movement came from the hallway.

"It's waiting for us." Several tears traced a wet paths down his cheeks. The night gathered around him, caressing his face with indistinct wisps of night greedily slurping up his tears. "It's the biggest fucking spider I've ever seen," Window continued in a soft voice, as if he was afraid speaking any louder might draw the attention of whatever was in the hallway.

From behind them came the sound of something being violently thrown against the wall, shattering on impact, its pieces clattering to the floor. Something solid struck the floor, followed by another, and another, each step getting closer as a faint clicking came from the gloom all around them.

Meat spotted movement against the floral wallpaper, only this time it wasn't a solid object. From a distance, it looked solid, up close he realized it was comprised of thousands of tiny bodies all scurrying in one direction as they flowed into the room from around the doorframe, vanishing into the thick gloom crowded into the corners of the room.

It's coming.

Meat grabbed Window's hand and freed him from the ebony tendrils wrapped around his body. From them came a sensation of longing that became a furious rage as they streaked across the room to ensnare their captive.

Meat leaned into his task, dragging an uncooperative Window to the door as the darkness reasserted its grip and tried to pull him back. They'd sworn a blood oath with each other as youngsters new to Bremo Bluff.

A promise to never abandon the other no matter how bad it got.

Meat was teetering on the brink of insanity as he struggled to pull Window from the creature's grasp. He wasn't sure when he concluded, or realized, what they faced was a creature straight out of a madman's nightmare. Connected as he was to its essence, with Window serving as a conductor joining the two, he understood with startling clarity what this thing was.

It resided at this spot, bound to the ground in which it lived, like a mutant fungi feeding on the occasional unwary traveler as time slowly unfolded around it. Where it came from was anyone's guess, it had always been. Watching impassively as man pushed back the wilderness to make room for the structures that would serve as homes and businesses to a growing civilization.

They'd forgotten the old ways as progress marched forward. Lost was the understanding there are places where the fabric between realities it at its thinnest. Where the past, the present, and the future all occupied the same space. Places shunned by those more attuned to their presence.

Quiet groves of eternal solitude the animals of the forest avoided in their daily lives. Strange creatures inhabited these silent places, beasts who could bleed across the lines of reality blurred by the blending of the past and present. The essence of legends and whispered tales shared over roaring fires, the basis of man's fear of the dark, for at night in these hushed places, the creatures roaming about bore little semblance to those man was accustomed to.

Modern man built up and developed the world in the name of progress. Replacing forests with wooden structures that soon gave way to concrete monoliths. Dark basements allowed this essence to survive, feeding on the despair of those who occupied these structures. Becoming the focus of whispered urban legends passed down from one generation to the next, the stories shared by the children who faced this thing.

It remained trapped in the dank chambers of the basement, surviving on the occasional stray child until the awakening brought it renewed life as terror washed across the land. It grew then, filling the cavities of the building, drawing sustenance from the fear all around it. Adding its own brand of terror as it focused its energy on a small band of children who took refuge with a man of the cloth. A man with secrets he'd successfully kept hidden from view.

Secrets now out in the open as the children, with nowhere else to flee, fell prey to his craven appetites. He taught them, and used them to satisfy his own desires, establishing a symbiotic relationship with the creature that fed a mutual need. The core group of children grew unrestrained by society, reverting to a primitive savagery as they added to their ranks the only way they knew how, by taking what they could not create.

In time, what the man wrought turned, as it naturally should, upon the creator.

39

"Don't be afraid," a familiar voice whispered as Gregory fell into the waiting arms of his wife. Comforted by her warmth, he allowed himself to relax for the first time since the day in March when the world was turned upon its ear. He was in the living room of the small cabin west of Richmond, but he knew that couldn't be right. They'd lost the place to another band of survivors. A group of men more savage than he could bring himself to be in the early days of the awakening.

Soft yellow sunlight flowed through the window, painting a bright square on the floor where Roscoe, their daughter's mutt, lay sleeping. He was a good dog, your average run of the mill Heinz fifty-seven running more towards spaniel, his black and white markings so reminiscent of a cow at times they referred to him as their miniature cow.

"Where's Shelly?" he said as a dark shape flashed across the window, accompanied by the distant squawk of a bird. Roscoe remained asleep, undisturbed, locked forever in a time and place that was a part of his memories.

"She's asleep in the back," Maggie, his wife, said.

Shelly was asleep all right. A sleep from which she would never awaken. He looked to the hallway at the back of the cabin, a short corridor leading to two bedrooms in the back. He could see no further than a few feet into the passage. Shadows filled the hallway and from them came a cold wind chilling him to the bone.

"No matter what happens," his wife said, "don't be afraid."

"I am," he admitted as he tightened his grip about her waist, afraid to let her go as he lay in her lap.

"We will always be here for you, waiting," she said.

The cold wind strengthened as the sensation of his arms about his wife's waist slowly slipped away and the room darkened. He struggled to remain where he was, clinging to the memory of his wife, his daughter, and the brief interlude of safety they'd experienced as the world came crashing down around them.

A vast expanse opened before him. An endless field beneath gray clouds that hugged the ground. Lightning flashed, dancing across the sky with wild abandon as thunder rumbled and the ground shook beneath his feet. The clouds slowly parted, driven back by an intense wind that shrieked with an eerie voice. As they dissipated the parted clouds revealed a towering stone structure that formed a Celtic knot.

The Trinity.

The once smooth surface was pitted and cracked. In places there were gaps where large parts of the whole were missing. The center trembled, bulging outward as something pushed from the other side, and shadows leaked from the widening cracks.

They're getting through.

A clawed hand emerged from the shadows as the center of the trinity collapsed entirely, leaving three points beyond to hold the dark forces at bay.

Points of pain erupted across his body, penetrating his flesh, covering him from head to toe as his consciousness of the world around him grew. He tried to move his arms only to discover they'd been bound, stretched out to either side.

The cold wind grew stronger as the sensation of something clinging to his shoulder intruded upon the past. He looked into his wife's eyes, so full of warmth and love. They shuddered, the image jumping like film knocked from its tracks, and her gaze took on a cruel indifference, darkening to a single black spot watching him with the odd detachment of an animal surveying its next meal.

What have I done?

He blinked, opening his eyes to be immediately overwhelmed with a sense of vertigo as the street running along the apartment building lay eighty feet below him. He looked down at his feet to find them tied to a steel post, his arms stretched out to either side of him, the wrists likewise tied as he hung over the edge of the roof.

He squeezed his eyed shut, terrified by the reality greeting him as birds cried out in raucous voices above him. He tried to tilt his head back, to see them, only a strand of wire held his head fast. From his left came the flutter of wings beating the air as sharp claws dug into the flesh of his arm.

He looked to the left, turning his head as far as he could. His gaze settled on the black eye of a crow watching him with indifference.

"Don't be afraid." His wife's voice came from the depths of his memory and he squeezed his eyes shut to escape the despair around him. Struggling desperately to rejoin her in a memory that would follow him to the grave.

Something pecked at his cheek, tearing the flesh, and he cried out in desperation, his shout sent the crow on his arm back into the air amid a flurry of flapping wings. It wasn't long before it returned, accompanied by others who fought among themselves for a good spot. Beaks shredded his cheeks as raucous cries surrounded his head like a halo. Pain flashed white hot as one of them found his eye and he screamed in agony as they battled over the morsel plucked from the cavity, ignoring his cries, confident that he could do them no harm.

"If thine right eye offend thee, pluck it out," the droning voice of Reverend Jacobs recited as the memory of stuffy mornings trapped in the close confines of The First Church of the Revival filled his mind. As members of the reverend's flock, he and his little sister, Mariah, attended every service with their parents.

With the memory of his sister came the guilt.

She called the morning of the awakening, begging for help. She lived twenty miles away, but Gregory was afraid as he packed up his wife and daughter to flee into the hills. He could have gone to get her, and maybe things would have been different. As it was, he didn't and never heard from her again. Except for in the middle of the night, when he lay awake, his sleeping wife beside him, as the guilt gnawed at the faith his parents worked so hard to instill in him.

"Don't be afraid," his wife's reassuring words whispered from the dark recesses of his memory, and he struggled to embrace them as his remaining eye was plucked from its socket by the crows gathered around his head.

In the resulting darkness a single point of light pulsed with a steady beat that matched the rhythm of his heart. It grew larger as the light intensified and details slowly emerged. A man with long hair and a beard appeared, the light coming from the halo behind his head. He recognized the man as the image of Jesus that hung on the wall of the classroom where he attended Sunday school as a child.

"I'm sorry," he whispered, "forgive me lord, for I have sinned."

The man smiled in response and Gregory felt a lifting of his spirit as the darkness receded to be replaced by a gray void. Voices whispered all around him, as if he were in a restaurant, or a theater, the steady undercurrent of life that stopped that fateful day in March. Among the voices he heard the familiar tones of his mother, his father, and his sister. They were joined by his wife and daughter. He'd come home at last.

Hands touched his body as he was moved, the wires binding his wrists were cut, and other voices intruded. He remembered the boys, and what they had come to do.

Jesus stood before him, his hands at chest level, holding an object Gregory had never seen before. It replaced the glowing heart depicted in the picture from his childhood and looked like the point where three circles intersected, with a fourth circle around them. The small part of a much larger picture

Three bound by a fourth. The though filled his mind as the object grew to overwhelm everything. The lines that at first appeared solid were in reality vast expanses of deep space filled with galaxies, one of which hosted his home. The outer circle held the darkness at bay, protecting those inhabiting the point where the three circles intersected. Like the goldilocks zone he'd heard about on the science programs he used to watch.

What does it mean?

"It's us, Meat, Window, we're here to save you." The voice sounded far away.

He didn't want to be saved. He wanted to stay with his family. He felt the muzzle against his chin, like a dream half remembered upon waking. Then he felt no more as the gray emptiness claimed him and he returned to his wife's arms, no longer afraid.

40

Emerging from the stairwell, Billie-Bob stepped into a wide foyer, a bank of elevators across from the door. The walls around him covered with drawings of crosses wrapped in barbed wire. From some of the crosses hung a crucified man. In many his expression was one of shame, in some he growled, his eyes glowing as he stared straight ahead. Scattered among the drawings was the same message repeated over and over in assorted hands, as if each person who lived here needed to publicly proclaim their belief.

Pain is love. Love is pain.

Sometimes love was painful. He thought of his mother, his brother, and everything they'd been through while growing up. Fleeing from one safe place to another, never able to let their guard down, always on the lookout for the next attack.

In the end, unable or unwilling to run anymore, she left them with her brother. Unaware he believed, no, he hoped she didn't know about her brother's twisted desires. If she did, would she have left them in his care? The question plagued him on nights when sleep eluded his grasp.

In addition to the proclamation, drawings of Celtic trinities were everywhere. An endless loop with no beginning or end, bound in the center by a circle. Three bound by a fourth. He'd have to ask Einstein what the image meant. Scattered among the Celtic trinities he spotted the triangles he'd seen at his Uncle's house.

The sound of approaching voices came from the stairs and he slipped into the hallway on his right as the door for the stairs opened behind him. He watched as three young boys, wearing loincloths made from drapes, passed across the foyer and vanished down the hallway. If he'd been another minute more, they would have met in the stairwell as he fled the creature from below. Though the boys were armed with what looked like rusty machetes, it would have been a massacre, with Billie-Bob's shots alerting the others to his presence.

As they passed from view, he became aware of the presence of another in the emptiness behind him. Reaching out to him on a psychic level as an icy touch caressed his mind and rifled through old memories, he'd rather remained forgotten.

With his mind's eye, he caught a glimpse of a cramped room lit by the harsh light of a small lantern. An older man sat with a young boy on his lap, a man he recognized as the uncle his mother abandoned him with. The image awakened old terrors as tears of shame and fear washed down his cheeks. Something whisked away the tears, slurping them up, and he was aware of a rubbery object caressing his cheek. It lived in the shadows around him.

Shots came from somewhere above him. The sharp reports severed the tenuous link between his memories and the emptiness throbbing with life all around him. He pushed himself to his feet, fleeing the memories, as he raced across the foyer to the stairs.

Pushing through the door he climbed the stairs through the darkness. Above him a door slammed open, followed by the sound of bare feet on concrete steps. He stepped back, the presence all around him once more, as if it was a part of the building itself. From above came shouts as the unseen group on the stairs appeared to be going up instead of down.

All Roads Lead to Terror

On the third floor, as shouts came from above his head, accompanied by the thrashing of a massive beast moving within the structure, he found the missing children huddled together in one small room. Eight of them, twice what was taken from the Bluffs, all young boys, and as he entered the room, they cried out in terror.

"It okay, I'm here to save you." He tried to comfort them. He recognized two of the children, Lex and Anthony, and called out their names. They came forward, their heads down, hands clasped together as they tried to give comfort or draw strength from the one beside them.

"Do you remember Anna?" Billie-Bob said.

The two nodded in unison.

"I like Anna, do you?"

Again, came a synchronized response.

"Can you help me?"

They nodded, looking up at him with wide eyes.

We have to get out of here. I'm going to lead you out of the building. Tell the others they need to stay with me and run when I tell them to."

They nodded and he sent them back to the group who gathered around them. They held a whispered conversation among them, several of them looking up towards Billie-Bob, their eyes falling to the pistol in his hand, and the rifle slung across his back.

It all started to make sense. He had not seen any girls because there weren't any. The drawings of the cross wrapped in barbed wire, the proclamations, they were sharing their guilt, expressing their pain, the only way they knew how. The triangles revealed the truth. At one time it served as a secret symbol, a call sign identifying the wearer as a member of a secret organization. A group his uncle belonged to before the awakening, a group of men whose tastes ran counter to what many viewed as normal and healthy.

Two years after finding The Bluff, he asked about the symbol, the image haunted his nightmares as the repressed memories of his time with his uncle struggled to come to light. First, he showed it to the Widow Winslow. She suggested he talk to Reverend Davis, who told him quite frankly what the symbol meant.

In the time before, the double triangle, as well as the Celtic trinity bound by a circle in the middle, served as a secret symbol for pedophiles to recognize one another. His uncle was a pedophile, and his mother left he and his brother in his care. Too young to fend for themselves, they became his victims.

"They roared their terrible roars and gnashed their terrible teeth and rolled their terrible eyes and showed their terrible claws," he whispered as the realization of what happened to him and his brother washed through him.

His uncle's voice replaced his mother's in his mind as the words whispered through his mind. He moaned as his understanding, coupled with a child's shame and terror, grew.

Pain is love, love is pain. His uncle whispered.

"Are you all right?" One of the children gathered touched his hand, bringing him back to the present and the danger they faced.

From above came the sound of screams and shouts. Shots reverberated through the building as some massive thing lumbered across the floor above their heads. The time had come to get loud.

41

From the hallway came the crashing sound of its approach, shattering walls as it manifested itself and lumbered through the interior of the structure. Screams of pain and terror drifted up from the floors below as the children who cared for this creature fled its unrestrained rage.

Window came away with an audible pop and they both fell into the hallway as awareness returned to Window's eyes. From the other end of the hall came shadowed movement. A slender tentacle rose up from the debris covered floor, whipping to one side it impaled its tip in the wall with a loud thunk.

Scrambling to their feet, they raced down the hallway to the stairwell. Meat glanced over the edge, into an inky well of darkness, spotting movement in the thick shadows filling the passage. It was their only escape.

Behind them, the approaching creature pulled its bloated bulk towards them. Meat caught a glimpse of swollen flesh covered by a rash of red protuberances like infected boils. They looked like they would pop at the slightest touch. Strands of a coarse black hair protruded from several of the infected bumps. The creature reached out with slender tentacles, groping blindly in the lighted stairwell, the tips twitching back and forth as they sought their prey.

The sight of the searching tentacles drove them up the steps. Coming to a door at the top they pushed through from one hellish nightmare into the next. They emerged onto the roof of the building, amid a forest of towering crosses from which hung the dead and decayed carcasses of men, women, and children. The temperature was unbearable, making it difficult to breath, the heat of the sun's rays amplified by the dark roof.

A flurry of flapping wings beat at the air, accompanied by the shrill cries of a murder of crows as they took flight, disturbed by Meat and Window's sudden appearance.

Among the dead, the dying cried out. One was the child who led them into the trap, next to him was the old man they'd seen at the apartment building. They spotted Gregory close to the edge of the roof, the surface covered by a layer of blood, gore, and bird droppings.

The smell overwhelmed them as they made their way through the forest of carcasses. Stopping at the old man, they carefully cut the barbed wire wrapped around his body and binding his arms and legs to the cross. Life imitating art, or vise-versa. Carefully, they lowered him to the gore-covered surface of the roof. The crows had been at him. One of his eyes was pulped and his face was covered with small cuts, some healed while others oozed fresh blood.

"You'll be okay now, old timer." Meat pushed himself to his feet. *Would he really? Did it matter?*

The door opened and one of those savage children stepped onto the roof carrying a makeshift pike. Meat drew his pistol and fired, the report sent the crows into renewed flight as the boy dropped to the surface of the roof, his weapon clattering harmlessly to the ground.

Another boy followed the first, and the roar of Window's revolver overpowered what he was yelling as he came through the door. He dropped to the roof next to the first boy.

A head peeked around the corner of the door and Meat placed a round into the door itself. The boy who hiding behind it dropped, clutching his stomach with both hands as he screamed in pain.

"Please help me," the child who brought them to this hellish place begged from his place upon the cross. A strand of barbed wire was wrapped around his forehead, the barbs piercing the flesh, blood stained his face in rivulet of red. So far, he'd escaped the attention of the crows gorging themselves on the bounty provided.

"Leave him." Window crossed to where Gregory hung from his cross. "Please, they made me do it."

Meat was torn between his desire for revenge and his need to protect those who could not protect themselves. The internal conflict stopped him for a moment as the crows circled in the air above, their shadows cast upon the roof, so close together they nearly blocked the sun.

Finally, Meat shook his head and walked away.

"Please," the young boy whispered through parched lips.

Meat surveyed the crosses covering the roof. From each one hung the lifeless carcass of a man, a woman, or a child. Confirmation, as if any was really needed, of the depths of the savagery these children had sunken into. Not one would warrant the slightest bit of mercy from him. They made their bed, and now they would die in it.

"Leave me alone," Gregory cried out as Window worked to cut away his bonds. They used barbed wire to bind Gregory's arms and legs, wrapping it tightly around his body, and he was bleeding from multiple points. Placed at the edge of the roof, he fared worse than the others. Both of his eyes were gone, the empty sockets leaking bloody tears streaking both cheeks.

"It's us, Meat, Window, we're here to save you."

"Leave me. I can't see anymore, I'm no good to anyone."

Using his wire cutters, Window cut away the wires binding Gregory to the cross. Carefully, they lowered him to the surface of the roof.

"Let me die." Gregory grabbed Meat's shirt in one bloodied hand. "I'm no good to anyone anymore. I've lost everything that's ever mattered to me. I want to die."

Meat glanced at Window, sitting on his haunches across from him.

"What do we do?" Meat said.

"Give him what he wants." Window pulled his revolver.

"It was fun while it lasted," Gregory said, "I'm ready to go now. Only make sure I don't come back."

Window nodded as he lowered the muzzle of his revolver and placed it under Gregory's chin.

42

In single file, they raced as quickly and as quietly as they could with Billie-Bob in the lead. Reaching the door to the stairwell, they stopped as Billie-Bob opened the door and leaned into the landing. Pushing the door all the way open, he motioned for the children to follow.

From above came the sound of pounding feet on concrete stairs, shouts and cries mingled with occasional shots Billie-Bob recognized as belonging to Meat and Window. He glanced over the railing, into the black emptiness of the stairwell, and knelt among the children who watched him with frightened expressions.

"I want all of you to hold hands with the person in front of you and the person behind you. It's going to be dark and scary while we run down the steps. Don't stop until I tell you. Okay?"

Several sniffles came as they nodded their heads. Small hands instinctively wrapped about others as they crowded closer to Billie-Bob. One of the boys looked over the railing, into an inky well of darkness, and cried out for his mother. The boy next to him wrapped his arm around his shoulder to comfort him.

"Let's go." Billie-Bob moved down the steps ahead of them.

From the stairwell above came cries of anger punctuated by the sharp report of a handgun and the sound of pounding footsteps. The children followed Billie-Bob into dense shadows. At the landing for the second floor, he stopped and waited while the rest of the children caught up with the main group, half of the group was missing. Above, a child screamed in a shrill voice.

"What are you doing out of your room?" A deeper voice responded to the scream and Billie-Bob turned back up the steps. Rounding the turn in the stairs, he came upon one of the boys from the savage band leading four boys back to the room he'd rescued them from.

Billie-Bob ran at the boy, pounding up the steps as the children cried out in alarm. The boy, who was at least twenty pounds heavier than Billie-Bob, turned as Billie-Bob slammed into him, driving him to the floor. Billie-Bob tried to straddle him and get his hands around his neck, the boy shoved him aside and climbed back to his feet, pulling a knife from his belt as he turned on Billie-Bob.

"I'm gonna eat your heart out of you." The boy slashed at the air with his knife. The children cowered against the wall as Billie-Bob smiled. Shaking his head, he pulled his pistol from its holster.

The children screamed as the concussion of the shot washed over them. The older boy's eyes widened in surprise as the round took him in the chest, the impact driving him against the steel door where he slid down to a sitting position, blood smearing the surface of the door behind him. He struggled to take a breath as his eyes locked with Billie-Bob's, and then he slumped to the left as he died.

Driving the children before him, Billie-Bob raced down the steps like a mother hen corralling chicks who wanted to go in every direction save the one she wanted. Reaching the landing for the second floor, Billie-Bob caught sight of movement out of the corner of his eye as another of the savage inhabitants of the building slammed into him from the left.

He'd obviously been hiding, waiting for them to pass before he launched his attack. Billie-Bob was driven against the wall, his pistol falling from nerveless fingers as his elbow rebounded from the block wall. The boy clawed at him, screaming unintelligibly, slashing at his clothes and flesh with his bare hands.

Billie-Bob managed to drive him away with his foot as the children huddled on the landing below. The boy launched himself at Billie-Bob, who was still looking for his pistol. He caught the boy by his arm, spinning him around, and drove him into the opposite wall with a whipping motion not unlike snapping the tip of a wet towel.

He couldn't find his gun.

He dropped to his knees, searching, as panic blossomed in the pit of his stomach. He crawled about, frantically searching the floor with his hands. His fingers brushed against the barrel, knocking it away from him, and it clattered down several steps before coming to rest. Before he could get back to his feet, the savage little bastard slammed into him from the right, driving him against the wall where he pinned Billie-Bob across the throat with his forearm.

Panic shrieked in Billie-Bob's mind as he fought against his attacker, kicking out wildly with little effect as he struggled to breathe. He was going to die, right here, in a dark stairwell in the middle of a dying city. The victim of a child turned savage by the death of society.

"I'm gonna eat your heart out of you," the boy whispered in his ear, his hot rancid breath washing across the side of his face as Billie-Bob turned his head away. A tremendous roaring filled his ears as his heart thundered in his chest, ramming against the prison of his rib cage. From the shadows cam the whispering snick of steel drawn across leather, and he spotted the faint shimmer of a metal blade in the boy's hand.

No.

In his mind, he returned to his uncle's basement, the memory unleashed by the panic washing through him. His uncle stood over his brother, his large hands clasped upon bony shoulders as he shook the boy with a wild rage.

Pain is love, love is pain.

No!

I've gotta stop him. I've gotta save Bobbie. The images in his mind stuttered like a film jumping its tracks, cutting to a scene of his uncle leading his brother to a small stage. He became aware of a hammer in his hand, heavy, the straight claws pointed at the floor as he carefully approached his uncle's back.

Love is pain, pain is love.

No!

I've gotta stop him. He grabbed the boy's wrist as the blade came close to his throat. It hovered there for a moment, trapped between the boy's need for vengeance and Billie-Bob's desire to live. The arm across his throat loosened as the blade drifted away from his face. He gulped in a lungful of air, giving him renewed strength.

Love is pain, pain is love.

No!

His uncle lay at his feet, Bobbie standing beside him, their hands clasped. A hammer growing from the back of his uncle's head as blood stained the floor around his face.

Love is pain, pain is love.

No!

He pushed back against the boy whose face was twisted into a snarl. His eyes burning with a predatory light. They held no anger, no remorse, only a savage need to spill Billie-Bob's blood.

He turned the boy's arm, bending his wrist until the tip of the blade was pointed at the boy's face. His eyes blanched when he realized things were not going as planned.

Billie-Bob twisted harder, fueled by fear, gaining the upper hand, turning the tip of the blade up as their interlocked grip slowly lowered between their bodies pressed close to one another. The boy's flesh was slick with sweat in the stifling confines of the stairwell. Sweat dripped into Billie-Bob's eyes, setting them on fire as he continued to struggle against the boys will. Under his clothes, his entire body was sheathed in sweat.

The boy grunted, bone snapped with a muted click, and the tip of the knife slipped in between his third and fourth rib. A look of surprise crossed the boy's features as the knife passed through his flesh, the tip seeking out his beating heart, caressing the struggling organ as it sliced through taut muscle.

He coughed as Billie-Bob rammed the blade home. The boy's lungs filled with blood and it spilled from his lips as his body relaxed and Billie-Bob lowered him to the garbage-strewn floor. The smell of fresh shit and spilled blood washed across him. Their eyes remained locked as the boy's life fled and the peace of death smoothed his features.

Billie-Bob crawled away from the boy's lifeless body, shaking from the exertion of the struggle, adrenaline thrumming through his body, his clothing soaked through with sweat. Coughing as he struggled to catch his breath. In his heightened state of awareness, the last of the walls he'd built around his past collapsed and he returned to his uncle's basement.

Somber lighting filled the basement, pools of deep shadows gathered around the edges. In one corner harsh white light illuminated a small stage. Jagged streaks of blood strained the walls, the floor of the stage, and the curtain that served as a backdrop. Photographic and video equipment waited, perched upon the spider legs of tripods. Something bad happened, the splattered blood mute testimony to the savagery that visited this quiet place. On the stage stood a small chair and the sight of it opened the floodgates of his memory.

He and his brother spent hours on the stage, together and apart, in various stages of undress. His uncle working the cameras beyond the harsh lights as the shadows moved in suggestive manners that awakened a sense of shame and self-loathing.

The tides had been turned.

His uncle lay next to the chair, his head turned to the side with a strange smile on his face, the handle of a bloodied hammer growing from the back of his skull. On the floor a single piece of jewelry glittered in the light, two triangles, one wrapped about the other, formed by a single line that gave it the illusion of three triangles stacked together. A piece of jewelry his uncle would wear no more. A simple piece that carried a much deeper meaning, serving as the unofficial symbol of an organization that had once existed in the shadows of a civilized world.

He'd saved his brother from the final degradation and everything from his past fell nearly into place. Billie-Bob brought his breathing under control and crawled to the edge of the landing where the children waited silently.

"Mr. Billie-Bob?" one of the boys said. He had come up the steps to stand in front of him.

"Yes," Billie-bob whispered hoarsely. His throat was going to be sore. But dammit, he was alive.

"Here's your gun." The held his pistol out to him.

"Thank you." Billie-Bob sat up and took the weapon, checking the load by pulling the slide back part of the way.

Using the railing, he pulled himself to his feet. At the same time, he became aware of the commotion on the stairs above them. Shouts and screams drifted down to them, shots reverberated through the shadows. He took the steps hesitantly at first, making sure he wasn't going to lose his balance and fall the rest of the way to the bottom. As his confidence grew, he guided the children down to the final landing that led to the foyer of the building, and the street beyond.

At the open doorway, leading to the street on the other side of the lobby, two armed guards stood with their backs to them. They were two boys, one on each side of the entrance, watching for external threats, not expecting trouble from within the building itself.

Motioning for the children to stay put, Billie-Bob crept across the gloomy lobby, staying to the shadows as he snuck up on the unsuspecting guards. When he was twelve feet away, both of them in clear view, one of them happened to glance back into the building.

He spotted Billie-Bob nearly on top of them, and with a cry of alarm, spun around, the muzzle of his shotgun coming up. Billie-Bob fired, the shot catching the boy in the chest and throwing him to the sidewalk. The second boy returned fire, the wad of shot whistling past Billie-Bob's ear, several of the pellets passed through the flesh of his ear, igniting a white-hot dagger of pain as blood splattered his shoulder. The pain touched off a rage that welled up from deep within and he charged the second boy as he struggled to reload his shotgun, the slide jamming in his panic.

Billie-Bob had no such problem as he bore down on his target. The boy managed to get the round into the chamber and the muzzle was halfway up when Billie-Bob's shot took him in the chest, throwing his body like a rag doll onto the front steps of the building.

With his head on a swivel, he checked for more attackers as he approached the doorway, glancing down at the two boys whose bodies lay on the sidewalk. Satisfied that they were safe, he motioned for the others to follow, and he led them onto the street, into the snarl of cars forever trapped in a traffic jam of the damned.

Reaching the other side of the street, he looked back at the building to see Window and Meat working their way down the side on a steel fire escape. Above them, a groupd of boys above threw anything they could find at them.

Billie-Bob unslung his rifle and steadied himself against the side of a car as he sighted through the scope. Young faces leapt into view, very close, and he chose the one furthest to the right. Gently he caressed the trigger, the rifle bucked in his hand as he rode the recoil, his eye firmly planted against the eyepiece.

His shot was low, spraying bits of concrete into the boy's face, forcing him to drop back. He must have knocked the sights off in his struggle.

Billie-Bob chose his next target, adjusting for the bullet's drop, and gently caressed the trigger. The rifle bucked in his hand and the boy's head exploded in a spray of blood, bone, and brains.

Billie-Bob kept watch over the empty escarpment as Window and Meat broke through a window to access the floor below where the boys gathered to worship their unholy god.

43

Time and neglect conspired against Meat and Window as they stepped onto the fire escape. The bolts that once secured the steel structure to the wall had loosened over the intervening years as the freeze thaw cycle worked on the mortar holding them in place. Without regular maintenance, the fire escape, designed to save the occupants in the event of a blaze, had become a potential death trap.

With their full weigh on the steel grate one of the bolt holding the platform in place pulled loose. The street was eighty feet below. If the fire escape failed there would be no coming back. Window fired at the door leading into the building, keeping their attackers at bay, for the moment. He couldn't stay long, the lack of enough ammo, and the way the fire escape threatened to fail forced them to hasten their escape.

The fire escape rattled against the wall as Meat and Window hurried down the steps. When they reached the landing, a brick slammed into the railing, sending a jolt through the whole fire escape, forcing them to pause. It was followed by a rain of bricks as the boys on the roof grabbed anything at hand to throw after them.

The report of a high-powered rifle stopped the rain of lethal objects and Meat glanced down at the street, spotting Billie-Bob and the children he'd rescued. They were safe, which meant they were now free to get out as fast as they could. Another shot echoed from the flat surfaces of the buildings around them as Billie-Bob kept the boys pinned down on the roof. It wouldn't stop them from coming down the central stairs, so they'd better hurry.

Window tried kicking through the glass of the window, his actions caused the entire platform of the fire escape to swing out away from the building. Nothing between them and the street below save the steel grate and eighty feet of air. Meat clung to the railing, his heart thundering in his ears as the platform swayed beneath them. When he was sure it was going to topple the rest of the way, throwing them to the pavement below, it reversed course and settled back against the wall.

"That was too close." Window clung to the railing with one hand as he pulled his revolver and fired into the window. Starburst patterns appeared in the glass, weakening it enough for him to kick it out, giving them access to the relative safety of the interior.

Inside, they found themselves at the end of a long hallway. From the ceiling above came the sound of wood breaking and fabric tearing. The ceiling's surface bulged downward as the sound intensified, cracks spreading across the surface of the drywall from the center of the bulge, and they both stepped clear as dust drifted down from the stressed ceiling. Drywall collapsed, pieces of shattered concrete, splintered wood and tufts of pink insulation fell to the floor.

As the dust cleared, they looked up into the glare of a furious eye that filled the opening that measured at least two feet across. The flesh around the eye was a stiff gray with patches of what looked like infected skin glistening with a reddish glow. The eye blinked, the crusted lid coming together briefly before sliding back to reveal a black iris surrounded by a yellow sclera criss crossed by jagged lines of blood red veins. Meat sensed the presence again, stirring up old terror, and he struggled to keep his sanity from sliding off into an endless abyss as the creature's alien presence probed his mind.

Shouts and the sound of running feet came from the stairwell at the opposite end of the hallway, breaking the spell the presence cast, and they both raised their pistols. The concussion of the shots fired in such close confines pressed against them as the eye vanished behind a crusted lid and a high-pitched shriek of pain and rage rebounded from the walls around them.

The sound jack-hammered into their skulls like a spike, probing the black depths behind their eyes, and sending out icy fingers of terror that washed through their bodies. They were in the presence of something that should not, could not, exist. Yet it did.

Black ichor splashed down from the shattered eye and they jumped back as it splattered the filthy floor. From the flesh around the eye, slender tentacles grew from the gray flesh, grasping the sides of the opening to pull the creatures mass through the hole. Several tentacles spiraled down to the floor, their tips blindly searching for them.

To the left of the shattered eye, a mound of flesh bubbled up. They watched in mute horror mingled with disgust as it opened to reveal another eye watching them with fury as smaller tentacles pulled its bloated body through the hole it created. The lid covering the center eye, the one they shot, opened, folding back to become lips around a tooth-lined gullet pulsing with ravenous hunger.

"There they are," someone shouted at the other end of the hallway.

Meat and Window were jarred from their morbid fascination, and with pistols at the ready, turned to confront this new threat. Two boys raced down the hallway towards them. One carried what looked like a machete while the other carried a short knife. They fired again, the boy with the machete dropping to the floor lifelessly as both rounds took him in the chest.

"I thought you were taking the one on the right," Window said as the other boy reached them. Meat stepped back, turning away as the boy tried to slash down at them. His momentum carried him past them, and Window gave him an extra boost by shoving him toward the shattered window behind them.

Before they could fire, the tentacles hanging from the ceiling dropped down and wrapped themselves around the boy's body. He screamed, slashing at the tentacles with his knife as he was lifted off his feet into the ceiling, his cries cut short by a wet crunching sound as blood washed over his shaking body. He dropped lifelessly to the floor, minus his head, as the tentacles resumed work pulling the bloated carcass through the narrow opening.

Meat didn't want to hang around to see what happened once it managed to get through, and they retreated to the stairs. Propane cylinders lay scattered all over the place. Nearing the stairs, three more boys emerged, armed with knives. No match for the weapons they carried, the three were quickly dispatched.

Another boy raced around the corner of the stairs above them. The sound of Window's pistol reverberated through the space as the boy was slammed against the wall where he slid lifelessly to the ground, smearing the wall with blood. Another boy stuck his head around the corner, jerking it back as a .44 round slammed into the wall where his head had been.

"We don't want to hurt you," one of the boys shouted at them.

Meat spotted the bloated thing drop from the ceiling at the other end of the hallway as those searching tentacles weaved back and forth in the light coming through the window. He gathered paper and wood along with some propane cylinders that were still half full. With the wood he created a pile at the base of the steps as the creature pulled its bloated body down the hallway towards them.

"We better hurry." Window's gaze alternated between the hallway and the stairs. Another boy poked his head around the corner and Window fired, clipping him. He cried out in pain. With the pile of debris waist high, Meat placed a number of propane cylinders on top and knelt down at the base. Using his knife and a flint, he sparked a fire in the paper at the bottom, blowing on it gently until the flames flared to life and greedily climbed the pyre of wood, filling the hallway with dense smoke.

Meat shoved another propane cylinder into the burning pile before he and Window raced down the steps to escape. From behind them, as they fled, came the sound of someone in pursuit.

Smoke filled the stairwell and the boys hiding there pushed back to the roof and raced across to the fire escape still clinging to the side of the building. Billie-Bob was waiting for them and, before they could retreat, two of them died.

As the bloated carcass neared the flames, the internal temperature of the propane tank reached a critical point. A high-pitched whistle was punctuated by the crump of an explosion that sent flames racing up the stairs and down the stairwell, enveloping those still fleeing to the roof, swallowing the approaching creature in cleansing flames racing the length of the hallway, igniting debris, and exploding through the windows at each end.

Fanned by the wind, the flames roared to life and quickly spread into the rooms and hallways of the floors above, trapping the boys on the roof.

Window and Meat reached the lobby and split off into different directions, fading into the gloom as the sound of pounding footsteps came from the stairs. The first boy emerged, carrying a shotgun he dropped as Window's shot took him in the throat. He was followed by a second who fared no better. Smoke billowed out of the doorway, flowing into the lobby as the distant sound of screams came from above.

Fleeing the building, Meat and Window joined Billie-Bob and the children who gathered in the shadows cast by the buildings along the main avenue. They watched as the flames consumed the upper stories of the building. Those trapped on the roof cried out in terror. Some opted to leap to their deaths, choosing a crushing impact with the pavement below over the greedy agony of the searing flames. Others succumbed to the smoke pouring from the upper levels. Some attempted to use the fire escape, meeting certain death as Billie-Bob calmly picked them off.

Meat's earlier resolve wavered as he was confronted with the brutality of their actions, and he was ready to pull Billie-Bob back and let the few remaining survivors escape when one of the walls of the building collapsed, falling in upon itself. The roof teetered briefly on the remaining walls before succumbing to the added weight.

A deep rumbling grew in intensity as the roof dropped into the flames and smoke, its impact weakening the already stressed internal structure as the floors slammed down, one atop another. Adding momentum where once there was none, the building collapsed within itself in a billowing cloud of dust and debris.

They took refuge behind several cars, a few of the children crying out as the world around them was plunged into an eerie dusk while the cloud of dust enveloped them. Everything became fuzzy and gray. The dust in the air made it difficult to breathe and they used their shirts over their noses to protect their lungs from whatever the dust contained. The rumbling rolled away into the distance like thunder as an eerie silence asserted its dominance. A few falling bricks punctuated the spectacular destruction of the building.

Meat lifted his head and peered over the edge of the car he'd hidden behind. Amid the clouds of dust hanging in the still air, he spotted movement, a dark figure lurched towards them, a twisted trunk of slender tentacles writhing in the air as its tips groped blindly for something, anything to grab onto.

It towered above them briefly before slowly collapsing within itself, unable to support its weight, falling to the pile of debris of the building it inhabited. Without the structure to provide shelter and support, it withered beneath a blazing sun.

Somewhere, a bird called out hesitantly, answered by another, as the sun slowly burned into the dusty cloud, confirming they survived. As the dust settled, they emerged from their hiding places, each of them covered by a fine layer of white dust.

Cautiously, Meat and Window approached the destroyed building while the others remained behind, watching from the safety of the rusted automobiles littering the street.

"What do you think it was?" Window came upon the twisted trunk of a number of those slender tentacles all wrapped about one another, lying upon the shattered remnants of the building as the sun slowly consumed it.

Meat shrugged. "No idea."

"I guess it doesn't really matter anymore now that it's dead."

"I don't think it's completely dead. Its roots are still in the ground. Like a plant, it'll probably come back."

"How can you be so sure?"

"I can't, but life is funny that way. It's persistent, like us."

"What about the rest of them?"

"Let em go," Meat said as cries of pain came from the shattered remnants of the building.

"You don't think they're a threat?"

"Not anymore."

Meat nodded as he surveyed the destruction around them. The day cleared as a ceaseless wind carried the last remnants of the dusty clouds away. Here and there they lay the lifeless bodies of the savage boys who inhabited the building scattered among the debris. Above them, the crows gathered for the feast, circling about, their shadows zipping back and forth across the ground.

"We need to get out of here," Meat said.

"You'll get no argument from me." Window followed Meat back to the group waiting for them.

44

The steady sound of the horse's hooves on pavement lulled Penny into a somnolent state. She could barely keep her head up as they followed state route 59. The sun above lay to the south, slowly warming the pavement, their shadows mingling with the gloomy depths of the forest on their right.

Aside from the accident they came across several miles back, forcing them into the forest to skirt around it, there was little sign of man's presence. It was as if he had ceased to exist, and they were the only survivors of a global catastrophe. Though the fantasy was compelling, she knew better. Mankind was still about, more savage than ever, if her current predicament was any indication.

At they neared rout 219 they came abreast of TJ's a convenience store at the intersection with route 219. Three cars sat in the lot, their paint faded from neglect, their windows filthy, hiding what lay within. Aside from the sense of emptiness, it could have been a typical day, in any of the days that had come before. A cold wind chilled her as she watched the cars. At any moment someone was going to step out of the store and cross to one of the cars. Out here, away from major cities and towns, the world continued to look as it had that day fourteen years before. On the surface the effects of the awakening were not as bad as in the cities. She knew better. Inside the store she was confident they would find the death stalking their species.

At 219 they turned south. Several abandoned cars sat in the roadway, their doors open, and in the back seat of one she spotted a car seat. She didn't want to look. She didn't want to know what had befallen an innocent child. But she couldn't stop herself. As the others moved down 219 ahead of her she approached the car. A blanket moved in the car seat and her heart climbed into her throat as her mind filled with images of babies in varied states of life, death, and the hell of the afterlife. She approached the car, powerless to stop herself, compelled to look against her will. She released her breath when she discovered the car seat empty. A breeze had probably stirred the blanket, *or the child's ghost.* A chill caressed her cheek at the thought.

Another sensation stirred, overwhelming her with the impression she did not belong. She nearly fell from the horse as strange images swamped her. She saw a group of children oddly dressed in loincloths. Their flesh covered with strange tattoos that made her sick to her stomach. More images followed, a city sparkling in the night, its lights reflected from the surface of a slow-moving river. Crosses wrapped in barbed wire, voices chanting in prayer, words written in fresh blood that slowly dripped down the wall beneath each letter.

This way to heaven.

Her stomach pulled itself tight in response and she wanted to vomit.

Images of more crosses filled her mind, each occupied by a decaying corpses. Low gray clouds moved slowly past the scene as flocks of crows darted back and forth across an angry sky. A terrified voice whispered a single word. *Wasta.*

What did it mean?

The images faded, but that sense of not belonging, of no longer being herself remained, stronger than before. Something touched that secret part of her soul, a part that did not belong. Ahead, the four horsemen stopped in their tracks.

Do they feel it too? She looked around, left, right, and back the way they had come. The sensation seemed to be coming from her left. She looked in that direction, at trees whose leafless branches reached for a cloudless blue sky. Skeletal hands lifted in prayer.

The horsemen turned around and came back. Without a word they passed and returned to route 59 where they turned east.

"Where are they going?" Jamie stopped beside her.

"They felt something."

"How do you know?"

"I feel it too."

"Bullshit, you're crazy." Jamie spurred his horse to follow and Penny followed as well. There was nothing else she could do. Nowhere else she could go. Their fates were entwined as intricately as were the threads of the past and the present.

They came to a sign on the right side of the road. Prison Area. Do Not Pick up Hitch Hikers.

On the other side of route 59 behind a high fence with barbed wire along the top sat a group of buildings. Another sign on the left marked the visitor and employee entrance for McKean FCI, deliveries were to enter at the next entrance. The horsemen turned down the narrow road, placing the fenced in buildings on their right.

Only a few cars were parked in the employee parking lot, with half that occupying the visitor lot. In front of the main entrance a circular road provided parking for the administrative staff around its circumference. The spots reserved for the warden, and assistant warden were occupied. Their vehicles, like the others they'd seen, had faded from exposure to the sun, their windows filthy. The surface of the lot was like every other road they traveled cracked with tall grass growing among the abandoned vehicles.

A small building flanked by wire topped fences stood at the edge of the circular driveway, dead leaves covered the front walk, piled against the glass doors of the entrance. Leaving their horses in the strip of grass the horsemen dismounted and approached the doors.

"Are we going in?" Penny didn't want to see the inside of the prison, but that sensation called to her and she found herself following the horsemen against her will. Something much stronger than her psyche had reached out to draw them here. Though trapped, unable to stop herself, she felt no fear. Whatever it was, it meant them no harm.

The peaceful outer appearance of the main entrance hid the destruction that had taken place inside. Dried blood was splattered across the floor and walls, desks and chairs lay upended, papers lay scattered all over the place. They passed through the main lobby, to the main doors that led to the admin buildings and the prison itself. The magnetic locks no longer worked, and the doors swung open easy enough. With their heads on a swivel they crossed the open space to the admin building. There they found more of what they discovered in the entrance. As well as the skeletal remains of several people. Pushing through to the prison itself, drawn by that irresistible need to see, they passed through the admin building, across another open area, and entered the prison proper.

The main building housed several tiers of cells, each occupied by the remains of a prisoner. Many had suffered greatly, slowly dying of starvation, only to come back as the undead, to suffer through the process of decay while trapped within an eight by ten cell.

They ignored the cells, crossing to a door marker utilities. This door was locked, but for an armed man, any lock was temporary. Beyond the door a stairwell led down into an inky well of darkness. It was from here the sensation emanated and without hesitation the horsemen plunged down into the emptiness.

Penny stopped, staring into the shadows, her psyche overwhelmed by the power calling to her. Against her will she followed the others, struggling every step of the way. It was a battle she lost too easily, and she darted down into the night, leaving Jamie alone in the utility room.

At the bottom of the steps they found what they were looking for, huddled in the shadows away from the light coming from above. They didn't like the light. It burned wherever it touched. She felt its presence on a purely emotional level. Its fear, its anger, its rage washed through her, out of her, fading away to be replaced by an overwhelming sadness.

It's weeping.

As she got closer more details emerged from the shadows. It lay curled into a tight ball, its flesh the color of night. There were no discernible features save the coarse irregularity of its skin. As her eyes adjusted to the dark, she realized the portion of the body she saw was only a small part of this creature. The rest of it vanished into the shadows of an open heat vent. It inhabited the nooks and crannies of the building around her.

Kneeling next to the body she reached out with one hand. The moment her flesh came into contact with the creature's the world she knew faded to nothing. She was alone with this being, connected by her touch, as a torrent of emotions washed through her. Fear, anger, and sadness came together into an image and Penny was no longer standing in the basement of a dead prison. She had been transported to a dingy, filthy, hallway filled with tattooed children. Two older boys stood at one end of the hall with guns. They were different in that they had no tattoos and a soft halo of light surrounded each of them. They were holding the group of children at bay as they made their escape. Smoke rolled along the ceiling as a high-pitched whine came from somewhere ahead. The whine was punctuated by an explosion, and roaring flames raced down the hall towards them.

She felt its agony as the flames washed over them and the window behind exploded onto the street below. Screams and cries of pan and fear came from within the building as a wall of fire filled the hallway, fanned by the wind its greedy voice crackled with a voracious hunger. The floor shifted beneath her feet as the building swayed. Gunfire came from outside. Screams came from the roof and a small body sailed past the window to the pavement below.

The sound of splintering wood came from somewhere in the depths of the building and the floor tilted to one side. The soft rumble became a roar that overwhelmed them. The ceiling collapsed and she was plunged into a terrible darkness filled with a tremendous roar as an immense pressure weighed her down.

She opened her eyes to the darkness of the utility room, the four horsemen around her as she gasped for breath. She reached out to catch herself and one of the horsemen stopped her from falling over. As the memory of what she'd seen grew dim, like a dream fading into the day, she realized she had seen two of the boys they sought.

"I've seen them," she said, pushing herself to her feet. "I know where they are."

The men looked at her, waiting for more.

"It's downtown..." the answer hid on the tip of her tongue. She'd seen the image before. City lights reflected from the surface of a slow-moving river, but she couldn't put her finger on where. No matter how hard she searched her mind for the answer, she kept coming up blank.

"I don't know," she admitted.

The horseman who attacked her at the Reverend's house grabbed her arms and she cried out, his grip like steel bands digging into her flesh. The pain helped to focus her thoughts and a memory she'd kept locked away for the biggest part of her short life emerged.

They were racing down the freeway, the wind in her hair, the roar of the motor blanketing every other sound. She sat in the passenger's seat of the car her dad was driving. The windows were down, the stereo blaring some heavy metal song from his youth. The road ahead was wide open, the sky a pristine blue, the prefect day for as short jaunt down a deserted highway. The car was a 67 Chevelle with a full blown 440 V-8 under the hood. For some the awakening served as a release from the dismay of a life without any real purpose. That was her dad. All he knew about was heavy metal music and muscle cars. The latter would have gotten him a good job if he weren't so stubborn and learned to work with other people.

He built the Chevelle after the awakening, when priorities were focused on things other than car parts and horsepower.

"Want a Pepsi?" He said as TJ's came up on the right.

"Sure," she said, regretting that decision now as she looked back on a life that could have been. Old man Timmons still ran the corner store and was willing to trade for anything. When they rolled into the lot there was another car next to the door and she remembered looking at it with a touch of trepidation. Maybe a soda wasn't such a good idea. But it was too late, her dad was already opening the door and stepping inside when loud voices came from the shadowy interior. Everything happened in a blur after that. There were shouts, followed by shots, and someone screaming. She remembered now it was she who had been screaming, her father dead at her feet as a man and a woman ransacked the place.

"What do we do about the kid?" the woman asked her partner.

"Leave her," the man said as he made his way to the door.

It was then she looked up at the counter, at the maps sitting in a rack. The one on top featured an image of a city skyline at night, the lights reflected from a slow-moving river.

"Richmond," she exhaled as the memory drove her to her knees and the horseman released his hold on her.

45

In half the time it took them to reach Richmond, they made it to Maria's house. Without the worry of being ambushed, they could relax their guard. Not entirely, but enough to pick up the pace.

The house was empty. Einstein's pack and weapons lay in the kitchen, and a troubling sense of despair settled over Meat as he read the sign all about them. The bed for two on the living room floor coupled with a musky odor could only add up to one thing. The discarded clothing draped down the back steps confirmed his suspicions as a new worry emerged. Was it consensual, or did Einstein force himself on Maria?

He kept these things to himself as he followed the steps into the backyard, noting the way the grass was bent everywhere they walked, one path led into the forest behind the house, another followed. He wasn't sure what happened, he suspected it was something to do with her being a girl, and he wouldn't rest until he found out.

"Where did they go?" Billie-Bob said.

Meat shrugged as he and Window stood with Billie-Bob. The children sat at the picnic table, exhausted and hungry after their ordeal.

"I'm gonna find them," Meat said. "You two go on and get the kids back to the Bluffs. I'll catch up later."

"I'm coming with you," Window said.

"I'd rather you went with Billie-Bob."

"It's not far to the Bluffs. I don't think he'll have any problems."

"It's not a problem," Billie-Bob said. "We shouldn't run into any more trouble. I'll let the kids rest a bit before we push on. You two go ahead, find Einstein and Maria. She was pretty neat."

The decision made, they parted ways with Meat and Window fading into the forest as Billie-Bob, surrounded by the children, watched them go.

The sign of Einstein and Maria's passage was easy enough to read, a broken branch here, a footprint in some soft mud there, a scuff on a stone. All of these things stood out to Meat, lighting the way as they moved with a predatory grace through the dense woods.

As the afternoon marched toward evening, they came upon the supermarket and stopped, watching the building for signs of life from the shaded protection of the tree line. Two armed men stood guard on the roof, rifles resting easy in the crooks of their arms.

A commotion came from the front of the store beyond their view. Motors ground to a stop, voices shouted as a group of people arrived at the market. Neither of them could understand what was being said, the lack of shooting confirmed whoever was in the market knew the people who arrived. The guards on the roof vanished from view.

"What are we going to do?" Window said.

"Try to get inside, see how many there are. Follow me." Meat stepped out of the tree line onto the pavement. Here the sign told him the rest of the story. Others came, a scuffle ensued, and someone was knocked to the ground. The twin trails of someone being dragged across the parking lot led to the building.

Meat and Window followed the trail to the far wall of the supermarket. Here the shadows were deepest, and Meat stopped, his back against the rear of the building. Window reached him, and together they made their way along the back wall as the sounds of a party came from inside.

At a loading dock, the overhead door stood partially open, leaving enough room for them to squeeze under. They emerged into a dock area piled high with mounds of garbage and the rotting carcasses of animals and humans. The stench was overwhelming, and it took every bit of willpower on Meat's part to keep from gagging as they carefully made their way through a twisted trail bordered by towering mounds of garbage.

From the dock area, they entered what was at one time the butcher's shop. Tiled white walls were covered with splotches and splatters of dried blood. Stainless steel tables were covered in the same, and the large double bowl sink overflowed with viscera. Above it a cloud of flies buzzed insistently. Bloodied tools lay about, left where they'd been dropped. From steel hooks along the back wall hung a number of carcasses in various stages of being dressed. Two human rib cages stood out among the animal remains.

He'd heard rumors of people turning to cannibalism to survive. Feeding on unwary travelers, the weak, and the infirm. Until now nothing was confirmed.

At the front of the butcher's shop a row of windows looked out upon the supermarket. At one time, shoppers could watch as the meat they purchased was prepared. Now the filthy windows were flyspecked and streaked with blood. Meat spotted the group who'd taken this place as their own.

Men and women had gathered around an open fire on the other side of the market. Lanterns hung from several spots, casting a pool of harsh white light that faded into a gloomy line along the perimeter. To the right of the group stood three gas grills, beyond them a pile of propane bottles formed a small hill. Two men worked at the grills while the rest sat in assorted chairs, drinking and smoking as a couple of women danced.

Outmanned and outgunned Meat slowly formulated a plan as he watched the cooks.

"If we could set off the pile of propane tanks, it'll wipe em out."

"And us too," Window said.

Two men appeared, Einstein between them. He looked like he'd been beaten, and Meat's anger stirred. *Where's Maria?* He watched the men escort Einstein to a third man who appeared to be the one in charge. He sat sprawled above the others in an overstuffed chair resting atop a platform.

"Look what we caught while you were gone," one of the men holding Einstein said. "Knowing how much you like boys, we saved him for you."

Meat tried to restrain Window, who jumped to his feet, ready to march out there. "Not yet," he said. "Where are they holding Maria?"

They watched in silence as the man in the chair reached up and pulled Einstein down onto the seat with him. Einstein struggled as the man tried to hold him down. Suddenly, the man jumped up with a shout of pain, his hand covering one side of his face. Einstein kicked the man in the balls, dropping him to his knees. The two who brought out Einstein beat him to the ground as the third man lay moaning.

Window ripped his arm from Meat's hand and pushed his way through a swinging door, passing through deep shadows to the group now distracted by the man beating Einstein.

His was the providence of the young, an aura of invincibility, the belief that anything bad would happen to someone else. It was the only edge he carried—that and surprise. Reaching the group, he stopped, and in a loud voice said. "That's my friend you're beating on."

Twelve pairs of eyes turned to Window, who stood beyond the light cast by the lanterns. One of the men peered into the gloom, straightened up, and shouted. "It's only a damned kid, get him."

Window's first shot took the man high in the chest, the power of the .44 slug driving him back several steps before he dropped to the floor.

Meat worked his way around to Window's right, coming up behind the two men on the grills. They stopped what they'd been doing, turning to watch the scene playing out between Window and the group. He didn't give them a chance to react. Covered by the sound of the pandemonium erupting after Window's first shot, he dropped both of them where they stood and waded into the group.

From outside came the unmistakable sound of a high-powered rifle and Meat recalled the two men standing guard on the roof. A few more shots came from outside before silence returned as shouts, screams, and gunshots filled the interior of the supermarket.

Window darted to the left, fading into the shadows as the other man who was beating Einstein fired blindly into the dark. Window's second round dropped him as he closed with the man who appeared to be the leader, lying next to Einstein's bloodied and bruised figure. His hands locked between his legs. The man looked up into the muzzle of Window's .44, and saw no more as the round shattered his skull.

Window knelt down next to Einstein and helped him to his feet. "Come on, we gotta get you outta here." Movement on his right caught his eye and he turned to confront a large bald man who was leveling his revolver on them. Window squeezed the trigger, and got nothing, the hammer falling on a dud, which was more common than not. Relying on scavenged ammunition sometimes resulted in unreliable loads as exposure to years of moisture took its toll.

Without hesitation, Window shoved Einstein to the right and drove into the bald man, who wrapped his arms around his body as they both went down. Once he was in close, Window pulled his knife from his belt and savagely stabbed the blade into the man's groin. The man screamed, relinquishing his grip as he tried to stop the dark red blood spreading across the front of his filthy pants.

The two dancing women cowered in a corner as Meat and Window waded into the group from two different directions. The women made their way to the front, where they slipped out and vanished into the growing night.

Meat caught a flash of movement from the corner of his eye, turning to confront an overweight man running at him with an axe above his head. He fired into the man's belly, the round not even slowing the man down, and was lifting the muzzle higher when the man's head exploded, accompanied by the sound of a high-powered rifle from the front of the store.

46

The battle was over as fast as it started, the dead lying around Meat and Window. The last of the group was drunk after a bout of heavy drinking and offered little threat or resistance as the pair worked their way through to the last man. Shooting each member of the group, without remorse, the image of the butcher's shop fresh in their mind.

When it was done, they helped Einstein to his feet. The sound of footsteps came from the front of the store and Meat spun around, his pistol at the ready as Billie-Bob emerged from the shadows. He expected as much after what happened with his overweight adversary.

"I told you to take the kids back to the Bluffs?" Meat said.

"I figured you guys might need some help, so I followed along."

"Where are the kids?"

"In the house. I left one of the older kids in charge until we got back."

"Did you get the two on top?"

"Of course."

Einstein groaned as he sat up, holding his head in his hands. His face bruised, one eye swollen shut, the flesh around it growing dark. He was gonna have one hell of a shiner.

"Where's Maria?" Einstein looked around at the dead bodies surrounding them.

"She wasn't out here," Window said.

Einstein pushed himself to his feet and ran to the back of the store. The others followed as Einstein pushed his way through the swinging double doors leading to the dock area. At the door to the walk-in cooler, he stopped and rested his head against it surface, swaying on his feet. He yanked on the handle, opened the door, and stepped inside.

"Maria?" he whispered as he vanished into the gloomy depths. From the little light available they made out the faint outline of Maria huddled on the floor in the back of the cooler.

"It's all right now," Einstein said.

"I know," she answered in a faint whisper. "Everything's going to be all right now."

"Maria." Einstein's voice trembled. "Maria," he shouted, his voice filled with a raw emotion making the others uncomfortable. "You can't leave me." His voice thick as he sobbed.

They waited silently, his sobs echoing from the darkness, sharing a sorrow each was intimately familiar with. After twenty minutes he emerged, his head down, his hands hanging at his sides.

"I'm sorry." Meat placed his hand on Einstein's shoulder.

Einstein looked at him, tears falling from in his eyes. "It isn't fair."

"I know." Meat gave his shoulder a reassuring squeeze.

From the depths of the cooler came the sound of someone moving, the rustle of fabric, the thump of flesh against steel. Halting footsteps approached as a shape slowly materialized. A ghost from the past emerging from the night. Maria staggered into view. Her flesh mottled and gray, cataracts filled her eyes, lending them a silvery glow. She worked her mouth in anticipation, saliva drooling from one corner of a twisted sneer. She was nude, yet they felt no desire for the twisted form presenting itself.

They stepped back as she staggered out of the cooler, her gaze fixed on Einstein, reaching for him with hands twisted into claws.

"You know what you have to do." Meat handed Einstein his pistol. "Give her peace."

Einstein looked from the pistol to Maria and back again as tears rolled down his cheeks. "I can't."

"It has to be you." Window took another step back, opening the distance between them.

Maria stopped and stared at Einstein. Her head tilted to one side like a dog will tilt its head when its owner speaks to it. Her expression smoothed. Even in her current state, she recognized Einstein, and waited for him to do what he must.

"I can't." Einstein pushed away the pistol in Meat's hand and turned his back on Maria. She stepped towards him, jerkily placing one foot in front of the other, her hands working in anticipation of tearing into warm, living flesh. At the last moment, right before her fingers touched the fabric of his shirt, she turned to Window.

Without hesitation, Window drew his revolver, his thumb pulling back the hammer with practiced ease, so fast to the naked eye his hand moved in a blur. From the hip, he fired. It was a shot he'd worked on throughout his short life, and the round stayed true to his aim, striking Maria on the bridge of her nose and plowing into her brain to end the mockery of her life.

Later, with time to reflect, they would wonder if, in those final moments, a small spark of what remained of Maria turned to the only one she knew would put an end to the miserable existence lying before her.

For the time, though, three of them watched as she crumpled to the floor, the fourth having done the only thing he could in the situation. Turn his back to let those more capable finish a task he could never complete.

47

With Billie-Bob serving as a lookout on the roof, they gathered all they could carry from the piles stacked haphazardly along one wall. They left the dead where they'd fallen, except for Maria. Einstein carefully wrapped her in bed sheets, insisting they bury her next to her mother. Meat shrugged in response. As long as Einstein carried her, he was good with it. His decision reflected no jealousy. It was simply a matter of survival.

They didn't know how long it would be before someone else showed up, if they even did. Leaving no time to worry over mundane details such as where someone should be buried. It was easier to leave the body for scavengers who would strip the bones of anything edible. At the same time Meat understood Einstein and Maria, no matter how he may have felt personally, shared something special and he chose not to argue the point.

Loaded with ammunition, and the few canned goods remaining, Meat lit a fire inside the building, and they vanished into the forest behind the market. They'd nearly reached Maria's house when a distant explosion confirmed the fire reached the stack of propane tanks.

At the edge of the forest in Maria's backyard, Einstein lowered her body to the ground as the others dropped their loads and settled down for a brief rest. From the house came a shout and Billie-Bob crossed the yard to meet with the children as Einstein started digging Maria's grave.

"Why don't you take a break before you do that?" Window said.

Einstein ignored him as he dug into the stony earth, sweat dripping from his brow, his gaze fixed on the task before him. He was obviously sore from the beating he'd taken, and the march from the grocery store. Yet his eyes burned with a fierce determination that drove him to finish the task before him. Meat suspected if they didn't do it now, Einstein might not be able to do it later, his emotions refusing to let her go.

Pushing himself to his feet, Window crossed to Einstein and gently pried the shovel from his hands. "Let me help."

Einstein stepped back and sank to a sitting position his legs crossed before him as Window struggled with the stony ground.

After fifteen minutes, Meat took the shovel and deepened the hole. The only sound was of the shovel striking the earth and birds in the trees around them.

"She liked listening to the birds sing," Einstein said.

Meat stopped what he was doing and wiped his brow with his forearm. "They give us hope," he said. "They're proof no matter how bad it gets life will go on."

The others nodded as Billie-Bob returned to the group. He was about to say something, stopping when the attitude of his friends became obvious. Instead, he took the shovel from Meat, and stepped into the widening hole to take his turn.

Though they'd been friends before their adventure, what transpired during their trip, and how they learned to rely on one another, helped strengthened those bonds. From this sense of camaraderie, they could all draw a measure of comfort, for by its very nature their friendship also offered hope for the future.

And in the end, when it was all said and done, hope was the only thing they had that could never be taken away.

Thanks for joining me on this brief foray into the world Meat and his friends inhabit. Their adventures continue in The Reaping Season. If you have a moment why not let others know what you think of my work by sharing a brief review.

Thanks,

Richard Schiver

August 2014

About the Author

Richard is the author of eight novels, three novellas, and a collection of short stories. His most recent works include Not of Us, a WWII creature feature published by Severed Press, and Cursed, a paranormal mystery centered on old legends that prove to be more fact than fiction.

During his life he has played a series of roles, husband, father, son, and lover, but his favorite by far is grandfather. He and his wife of twenty plus years have raised four children and helped raise eight grandchildren. They provide a secure home to a yellow lab named Max.

His wife, Dena has experienced firsthand the exasperation of living with a writer whose mind tends to wander at the most inappropriate times. Yet she manages to keep his feet firmly planted on the ground.

Richard can be found online at:

Facebook: http://www.facebook/RichardSchiver

Follow Richard on Twitter: @RichardSchiver

Bookbub:https://www.bookbub.com/authors/richard-schiver

Written in Blood is Richard's personal blog where he shares his writing, and whatever else might strike his fancy when time permits. http://www.richardschiver.com

He can be contacted directly at rschiver@gmail.com and would be delighted to hear from you.

9 781951 552060